THE
TROUBLE
WITH
ALICE

Olivia Glazebrook

THE TROUBLE WITH ALICE

Published in 2011 by Short Books

Short Books
3A Exmouth House
Pine Street
EC1R 0JH

10 9 8 7 6 5 4 3 2 1

A CIP catalogue record for this book
is available from the British Library.

ISBN 978-1-907595-15-8

Printed in Great Britain by Clays, Suffolk

For Clare

Part One

1

Through the yellow air the car fell, and then out of the sunlight and into the shade of the mountain. In the air it turned over, catching the light with a glint and a flash before – *bang* – it hit the ground and careered the rest of the way down the stony hill on its roof.

It continued to make a sound like something being torn in half as it skidded down the side of the valley but in the end, with a crump, the rear end hit the bottom of the hill, and it stopped dead.

Then there was silence again, and everything was as it had been before in the empty desert valley except for the addition of a Mercedes-Benz 5-door saloon, lying as helpless as an upturned turtle. Its wheels pointed skywards; its grey underbelly was bared; it lay half propped at an acute angle. Its boot was wedged into the ground and its bonnet pointed up towards the twisting mountain road from which it had tumbled.

Nothing moved. For a moment nothing stirred. Then

came the sound of something – someone – scratching; scrabbling to get out. The front passenger door opened and a man fell on to the dirt limb by limb like a contortionist from a box, struggling with the seatbelt and the heavy car door which slammed behind him when finally he slumped on to the pink dust. He lay there coughing, then he tried to stand but instead slid on his back down the remainder of the slope to the flat ground. For a moment he was still, his shirt all rucked up round his ribs. Then he turned over on to his hands and knees and straightened up inch by inch, testing his legs and using the car to support himself. He stood. With a gentle hand he cupped one ear and shook his head.

On the other side of the car a second man emerged: the driver. He dropped out on to his backside and slid straight down to the ground. His eyes were wide; he trembled all over as he too attempted to stand. His knees buckled and he had to lean on the car. He was too shocked to speak.

The first man turned on him and shouted, 'You bloody little man, Karim! What have you done?' Then he started coughing again.

'Mr Kit, I'm so sorry, sir, I…' Karim spread his quivering hands, upturned, in a gesture of helplessness. Then his eyes darted to the car and said, 'What about the lady?'

Kit looked at him, stupid for a moment, and then said, 'I don't know, Karim, Christ! I don't know.' He turned to the car and pulled at the back door, but it would not open. He tugged at the handle again, saying, 'Alice? Alice? Can you hear me?' He crouched beside the window, tapping on it, pressing his face on the tinted glass. 'I can't see anything,' he said. He dragged himself up the dirt slope, wrenched open the front door and crawled back into the seat – now an upside-down cavity – from which he had emerged. As he got into the car the door fell shut on to his legs and he let out a yelp of frustration before peering into the back of the car and pleading, 'Alice?'

There was no reply, just silence, and whether it was a live silence or a dead one he could not tell.

'Oh God, oh Christ, Alice, Alice,' said Kit, getting back out of the car, slipping over, standing up again, pulling at the back door, begging it – *'Please, please,'* – thumping it, and eventually smacking the window with the flat of his hand. Then he slid down the slope and dragged himself up the other side of the car to tug at the back door on the driver's side. It too remained sealed. Abandoning it, he wriggled into the car again via the front and crawled between the seats into the back.

Inside the Mercedes it was hot, dark and quiet. There was a stink of fuel and burned grit that seemed to cut at the inside of Kit's throat. Across the back of the car, wedged between the roof and the rear headrests and looking like a bundle of clothes, was Alice. It seemed too small to be her, Kit thought. She was folded up, her neck and shoulders pressed against the quarterlight window. Kit could not see her face or any part of her head, just her hair, which made him feel a surge of panic. She faced the back door, away from him, and she was quite motionless – beyond motionless, in fact: she was as still and quiet as a fly trussed in a web.

Kit saw that he could not get her out without tugging at her and unfolding her from her little bundle. He did not think it wise to pull at her shoulders from behind in case she had broken her neck. Instead, he flipped at the door handles with his fingers and then touched her shoulders, her back and her calves with his fingertips, imagining that she might turn her head and laugh, *What are you doing, my love?*

Between her shirt and her shorts a little bit of the bare skin of her back was revealed. Kit pressed his fingertips against it, as if he had never touched her before. He thought, *This will tell me whether she is alive or dead. Surely if she were dead I would be able to tell?* Surely that was a little beat, a pulse, that he could feel beneath his fingertips?

He let out a sob, 'Oh, please, Alice...' But she did not move. He was struck by panic and claustrophobia. He scrabbled backwards out of the car again and slipped down to the ground.

Karim was half sitting on the upturned back end of the car, fingering a cigarette out of his shirt pocket. Kit rounded on him, snarling, 'Don't you dare!' Karim stared at him and Kit held his tongue and caught his breath. *What if I need this man to get out of here?* he thought. He spread his hands and said, 'Look, I'm sorry but there might be fuel around... We don't know... Let me think for a minute.'

Karim said nothing, but he put the cigarette back in his pocket. Kit rubbed his head and then asked, 'Where's your telephone?'

Without speaking, Karim opened the driver's door and rummaged about in the front of the car. He re-emerged with a mobile phone and held it up, frowning at the screen: 'No signal.' He and Kit both looked up with intimidated faces at the dishevelled, rocky slopes which surrounded them.

They had ended up at the bottom of a little valley, one amongst a thousand, perhaps, or ten thousand, in their surroundings. From the air this landscape would look like a scrumpled brown paper bag or an unmade bed, for it is desert, and featureless but for its contours: steep-sided troughs, shaded now in the afternoon, and sharp-edged, red peaks.

The Mercedes had been descending a road which twists through the mountains that lie between Wadi Musa, where the ancient city of Petra is, and the flat, wide valley, Wadi Araba, which contains the Dead Sea. Kit recalled, with a mounting sense of alarm, that their narrow road had had neither markings nor signposts; that only one or two cars had passed them; that they had not driven through any villages since they had left the outskirts of Wadi Musa.

The accident had happened in a second. Heading westwards with the sun shining into his eyes, Karim's attention had been diverted by his mobile phone. He wanted to send a text message: the screen had told him he had no signal but he repeatedly pressed the 'send' button, his eyes flicking from phone to windscreen and back. Kit had been asleep in the passenger seat and Alice, feeling sick, had been lying down across the back. She had been staring, with eyes dulled by nausea, at the ceiling of the car. Neither had seen Karim look up from his phone (clasped between his hands on the steering wheel) to find a tight corner close in front of him, closer than he liked. They had been alerted by his exclamation, and by his violent – too violent – tug at the steering wheel. The car had slipped – you could not even have called it a skid – on the loose surface as they were wrenched away from the corner. Karim, cursing again, had swung the wheel the other way and that had been enough to send them gliding towards the edge of the road. Kit woke with a start, thrown against the passenger door, and glanced sideways at Karim in alarm. Alice had said 'Oh!' in a surprised voice, and attempted to sit up in the back, to steady herself with a hand on the headrest in front of her. Karim tried to correct his steering for the third time, plucking with panicking hands, but one of the car's back tyres drifted off the edge of the road and the car dipped; hung backwards; tilted, and then tipped. One wheel over the edge became two.

Alice had clutched in terror at the empty air of the interior; Kit had turned his head towards her. The slip had turned into a spin and then the car had turned over in the air – quite slowly, to those within, but to an observer (if there had been one) it would have happened in a glimpse, a flash of metal – before hitting the ground with its roof, bang, and then circling, sledging, skidding and sliding one, two, three hundred feet down the rocky slopes until it could go no further.

'Karim,' said Kit, squinting up at the hillside above them, 'you'll have to go up there, somewhere, and phone for help. Alice is pregnant. We can't move her; we have to get a doctor here. She might be bleeding internally, or something, I don't know...'

'Yes.'

'Find someone, phone for help, something. I can't leave her. She might wake up. And then wait, wait on the road, so you can show them where to come. Don't go anywhere.'

'OK, yes.'

But he continued to stand there, not doing anything, not moving.

'Karim! Go!'

'OK, I'll go,' Karim said. But he hesitated, and then said, 'But maybe, maybe you should go? And leave me here? You can stop a car up there, on the road –'

'Fucking well do as I say!' shouted Kit. 'Get up that fucking mountain! Do you think I'm going to leave her here, with you, alone? After what you've done already? What if she wakes up? What if she dies?' His voice was feeble in that wide open space.

Karim said nothing more, but turned to the hill and started trying to walk up it. It was hard going: the slope was covered with loose scree, and there was nothing to hold on to. Within a few moments he was drenched in sweat.

From beneath, Kit watched Karim's slow progress up the stony hill, seeing his shirt turn translucent with sweat and cling to him in patches. Kit felt rage suffuse him from his toes to his fingertips as he stood and watched each hobbling step the other man took. For every step up, Karim slipped back down half as far. The only sound, the diminishing scrape of Karim's sham Italian loafers sliding downwards on the stony ground, tormented Kit.

Sweat trickled down his ribs, out of his hair and into his eyes. Silence engulfed him like a dense fog. He swallowed and for nothing more than the comfort of the sound of his own voice called up: 'Don't forget where we are! Don't go too far away!'

Karim either did not hear or took no notice (*That bloody man*, thought Kit with savagery,) but continued his dogged struggle up the valley wall, his head bent with purpose to his labour, his fingertips clutching at the dirt.

With Karim out of sight, Kit felt more alone, somehow, than if Alice had not been there at all. At present she inhabited a different world, and he envied her.

He turned and looked at the car. 'Alice, you've got to wake up,' he muttered, but he realised as he said it that in fact it would be better if she didn't, until help had arrived. To regain consciousness trapped in that place would terrify her. And the baby... how could it survive such a thing? Kit swallowed. He had no idea what to do now. He looked at the sky, the ground and his shaking hands, and then pulled open the car door again and wriggled back inside.

The door wouldn't stay open. It kept falling shut on to his shoulders and then on to his legs, which for some reason made him angrier than almost anything else. He wanted to tear it from its hinges and hurl it into space.

'Alice? Can you hear me?' he whispered. Something in the car was clicking, or ticking, and then it stopped. 'Alice?' he said again. He licked his lips. 'Please? Come back.'

He got out of the car and slipped to the ground beside it. What the hell was he going to do now? *Dear God*, he thought, *I'll do anything if you'll get me out of this, I really will; I promise I'll never do anything bad.* To his surprise tears burst from his eyes. He shut his mouth tight and rubbed at his eyebrows with his fingers, frowning to make himself stop crying. 'Please make sure she's OK,' he said. 'Please.'

Panic ignited in his chest and although he tried to smother it, taking deep breaths, tears squeezed from his creased-up eyes and refused to stop. He gasped and clutched for breath; his mind leapt and plunged like a Geiger counter. He tried to level it by steadying his thoughts: how could he get her out? How could he wake her up? To get help, to get her out of the car, to get her to a hospital, and to get both (no: the three of them, including the baby) home? A terrifying and insurmountable challenge! The difficulty of it! How could it be possible? Thoughts scorched across the surface of his mind and he tried to beat them back but he was overwhelmed and so he gave up and sobbed with his mouth hanging open, his hands over his face, and spit and snot spooling into his fingers.

Then he stopped and rubbed his face with his shirt, and stood up. 'I must be practical,' he said aloud, wiping his fingers on his trousers and passing a hand over his face and head.

Karim must have got back to the road by now. Once there, he would telephone for help. How long would it take to arrive? An hour? Two? Kit felt panic clutch him again as he wondered how they would get her out, when they came… How would they get a stretcher down to the car from the road…? *Calm, calm, be calm*, he told himself. He looked around to see if there might be another way into their valley, a way that a car could take, but it seemed to be a neat, enclosed bowl. *When will it get dark?* he wondered. He looked at his watch: five o'clock.

Seeing the watch face seemed to root his experience

in an undeniable, appalling present, and fear fluttered inside him. He could tell by the softening light that the sun was beginning to set; he could feel on his bare arms the temperature begin to cool. His sweater was in the car boot: unless he could turn the car back on to its wheels it might as well be on the moon for all the use it could be to him.

He thought to himself, *It all comes down to Karim.* Then he thought, *Perhaps Karim will not come back.*

This thought set off another blaze of panic and he tried in desperation to put it out, but again his mind was alight and leaping. *What then?* he thought. *What if I have to spend the night here? Here in the car, with Alice unconscious? And what if she dies?* 'No, no, no,' he said, rubbing his head and pacing the dirt.

There had to be a point at which it became acceptable to leave Alice here and climb up to the road to find help. He could not sit here in the car through a long, dark night, not doing anything, not knowing whether Alice would live or die, and perhaps have her die right next to him. He could not.

Amongst his feelings of terror, panic and distress, Kit had room to feel astonished that something quite so dramatic, so impossible, so *wrong* could have happened. They were on a weekend break, for heaven's sake, a last -minute dash to the sun. Moments before, they had been looking forward to two nights at a plush hotel on the Dead Sea, having spent the two previous nights at Petra.

And now Kit was at the centre of a nightmare, a nightmare of untold proportions, with no knowable conclusion. If they survived, and the baby too, they would tell the story to their friends, sitting around their kitchen tables with wine and cigarettes, and everyone would say, 'My God, you were so lucky.'

If they survived. If. The word struck like a clock in a dark hall.

To distract himself, Kit hurried his thoughts along. So: it was five o'clock. If Karim did not appear again soon, in an hour perhaps, Kit decided he would climb out of the valley and up to the road. He would have to go before the landscape was plunged into a purple darkness, when he was able still to see his way.

Glad of a plan (of some description at least) Kit exhaled and put back his shoulders. Then he climbed back into the car and crouched there.

It was very hot and uncomfortable, and the air was sour. He held his breath and listened for Alice's breathing. He thought he could hear it, very faint, as if she were in a deep sleep. If he could have silenced the sound of his own blood rushing through his ears, then he might have been able to hear her better. He tried to remember everything he had ever learned about first aid but he was distracted by a raging thirst and by the idea that there might be something to drink in the glove box.

He had meant to get more water when they stopped for lunch, but the hotel had seemed so near. 'We'll be there in two and a half hours,' Alice had said. 'Karim told me.'

Kit had thought, *Well, that's no time at all. I'll wait, and have a proper drink at the hotel.*

He fiddled with the catch of the glove compartment until it flipped open and everything inside fell on top of him:

a can of Coke (full), two water bottles (empty), a Bic lighter (green) and several packs of Marlboro (red).

Kit picked up the can of Coke and unwrapped one of the packets of Marlboro. He inhaled the smell of fresh cigarettes and said aloud, 'Sorry, Alice.'

He imagined what she would have said: 'Oh, Kit, you are hopeless... You don't really want one, do you?' It was almost as if she had spoken.

He took a cigarette from the pack, got out of the car and used the empty water bottles to prop the door open. He walked twenty feet away and crouched on his haunches in the pink and white dust.

It was cool, now, and neither light nor dark: a mellow dusk. The landscape around him was softly defined; it seemed less harsh, and Kit felt comforted. The tops of the hills around him glowed orange, lit by the sinking sun, but quite soon both he and they would be suffused by indigo and then turn to a violet dark.

He opened the Coke can and a geyser of Coca-Cola exploded all over him. He gulped at the remaining half-can. His hands and face were now sticky with sugar and he wiped them on his shirt and lit the cigarette, taking a deep inhalation and setting off a coughing fit. He had hardly smoked since Alice had moved in. This one was disgusting – it felt like a horrible punishment – but he puffed away at it with determination, thinking it appropriate. But, *Oh no*, his head started to swim and he rocked back on to his heels, *Shit*, and then landed on his backside on the ground, weak and limp. *That wasn't such a good idea,* he thought. He felt limp; helpless; unable to hold himself upright. He lay flat on his back and reached out to feel with his fingertips the loose dirt, sand

and small pink stones on the surface of packed earth.

The ground tilted and he felt a wash of nausea. His feet seemed to have been swung above his head by an invisible hand. He dragged himself into a sitting position and stubbed out the cigarette, then pulled his knees up to his chest and hung his head between them. He wanted to giggle, then to weep. *This is not good*, he thought, ashamed. He heard a roaring in his ears, as if he were standing next to a waterfall, and the queasiness intensified until he gave a little moan and his mouth filled with drool. He gave up trying to recover himself and toppled over on his side to lie on the ground with his knees drawn up to his chest. His mouth was a little bit open, and to shut it seemed to require an effort quite beyond him. The roaring in his ears was overwhelming. A grey fizz like the seething grey mash on an untuned television screen began to wash into the perimeter of his vision until only a grey whirlpool remained, gradually shrinking, and then there was nothing but a pinpoint of daylight remaining in the centre of his vision, and then that too was engulfed by the wriggling grey worms, and Kit fainted dead away.

2

They had wanted a weekend away before Alice was too pregnant to enjoy herself. At eighteen weeks she had stopped being sick all the time, still looked 'normal', as Kit put it, and hadn't become 'weird'. ('When are you going to start acting all weird?' had been his question to her one morning.)

'Lucky you,' said Kit's friend Rob to him gloomily. 'Naomi was a fucking monster, from day one. And in fact, she's never stopped. I kept waiting for the pre-pregnancy person to come back, and she never did.'

'Somewhere hot,' Alice had said, talking about the weekend away, 'but not too long a flight. Somewhere I can swim, but not a pool. I hate swimming in pools.'

'Do you?' Kit said. He thought it over. 'I suppose we've never had that sort of holiday.'

'We've never had any sort of holiday. Except LA, for the show.'

'*That* fucking place,' began Kit.

'OK, OK, don't start.'

This conversation was taking place in bed, in a nest of the weekend newspapers. Kit, turning the pages of the Travel section, had said, 'Maybe we should go away for a few days. Don't you think? While we can?'

Alice had put on the sepulchral voice she used when Kit said something about how there would be nothing to look forward to after the baby: 'Of course, because *we'll never go on holiday again once we have a baby.*'

'Oh we will,' said Kit. 'Just not together.' He was only half joking.

'Pig,' said Alice. Now she was only half joking.

After a pause she said, 'But I thought you hated going abroad. Why did I think that?'

'Well, I don't like holidays,' Kit replied, 'but a week-end is different.'

'I *love* going away,' said Alice, picking crumbs off the front of her vest. 'You choose somewhere. Surprise me.'

But he couldn't surprise her because she had so many criteria. In the end they narrowed it down to the Middle East (hot, near, and then Jordan (warm sea, no fighting). Kit fetched his laptop and they found a deal: a flight to Amman, a hotel in Petra, another (five-star luxury, they read) on the shore of the Dead Sea, and a flight back.

'What is Petra?' asked Alice, looking over his shoulder.

Kit turned his head to see if she was joking, and saw that she wasn't. He swallowed the thought that struck him (*How can I be having a baby with someone so ignorant?*) and said, 'It's an ancient city, carved out of the rock. Hang on, I'll Google it. There's a very famous building, it's in a canyon and its façade is cut out of a cliff face. Here's a picture… There you go.'

'Oh my *God*, I know: it's in *Indiana Jones*,' she said. 'I always wondered where that was.' Kit must have looked blank, because she added, 'The one with Sean Connery.'

'I never saw it.'

Alice looked at him in amazement. 'You've never seen *Indiana Jones*?'

'Not that one. I saw the first two.'

'Wow,' she said. Kit felt irritated, especially when she mocked him, saying, 'It's your age, pet.'

There was one sour note before they left, sounded by Alice's sister Emmy, who said, 'Why do you have to go abroad? It's so stupid and pointless. Go to a hotel in the Lake District for the weekend if you must go away. Don't go to bloody Jordan. What if something happens? You'll have some idiot poking at your girlie bits with a spoon.'

Kit found Emmy one of the most testing things about his relationship with Alice. She was much older than Alice – more his age than hers, in fact – although it didn't feel like that; it felt as if she was older than him too. She disapproved of him: she had known him a little bit in the old days, when he had been wild. What's more, she had all but brought Alice up herself, so there were issues. She was protective to a fault and, Kit flattered himself, a little bit jealous.

Emmy chose the night before they left to say her little speech. The three of them were having dinner at a Chinese canteen in Soho where the sisters had been coming for years. Now they took Kit as if it was a marvellous treat for him, to be included in their little ritual, but in fact he preferred something more expensive, with napkins that were not made of paper and a menu that came in English. Sometimes Emmy's desire for authenticity seemed to make life more unpleasant than it need be.

Alice was inclined to go along with Emmy – she had all her life – but she was irritated by these comments. Kit had noticed, with some satisfaction, that since the pregnancy Alice was more likely to disagree with her sister, to say no to her and to rebuff her admonishments. Now Alice frowned as she loaded her pancake with shredded duck. 'People do go on aeroplanes,' she said, 'when they're pregnant, all the time. Right up to thirty-five weeks.'

'It's not the plane, dummy, it's the hospital the other end.'

'God, Emmy, shut up, will you? You're being boring. Make her stop, Kit.'

'What does *he* know?'

Kit, tired, looked up from his plate of what seemed to be fried duck fat covered with jam, and said, 'Look, Emmy, give it a rest, would you? It's four days, for God's sake. We'll be back on Tuesday. Can we talk about something else?'

'OK, OK, sorry,' said Emmy, waving hoi-sin-stained hands in defeat. 'I expect I'm jealous. I've got to work on Saturday and Sunday.'

'What is it?' Alice asked.

'A wedding. And lunch the next day.'

'Oh, how sweet,' said Alice, her head on one side.

Now Kit and Emmy exchanged glances. They shared similar views on marriage, while Alice was 'so soppy it's ridiculous', as Emmy said, and cried over weddings even when they happened in *EastEnders*.

'They're not sweet at all,' said Emmy. 'It's second time round for both of them.'

Alice would not be put off: 'It is – if anything, it's sweeter.'

Emmy rolled her eyes, and Kit laughed and put his hand over Alice's on the table. '*You're* sweet,' he said.

In the taxi on the way home Alice turned from the window and said, '*Are* we mad to go away? It will be all right, won't it?' Kit felt her hand steal across the seat and into his. He squeezed it.

'Of course it will. It's nothing – Emmy's cross because you're having a holiday. She needs a boyfriend.'

'Men are so irritating! You always come out with that, and it's not true: she doesn't. Emmy's *vile* when she has a boyfriend. She's only just got rid of the last one, anyway, as I've told you a million times. I wish you listened to a single word I said.'

'I can't be expected to remember everything,' Kit countered with indignation.

'No, but some things? About me? Surely?'

'Don't be peevish. You're always like this after we see Emmy. You're channelling her.'

'*Channelling?*' Alice laughed. 'Where did you pick that up?'

'I read your *Grazia* in the bath.'

Alice giggled and leaned over to kiss him. '*Channelling,*' she mocked him. Then she murmured into his ear, 'I love it when you talk teen slang.'

When they got home Alice wanted hot chocolate and

so Kit went upstairs to bed and left her in the kitchen, surfing on the computer while the milk warmed up. He was almost asleep when she came into the bedroom.

'According to the website,' she whispered, 'I might feel the Bean kick any time around now.'

Kit rolled on to his back. 'Why are you whispering?'

'In case he's asleep.' She put her cup down beside the bed. They were both quiet for a moment.

'Well, let me know if you feel anything,' Kit had whispered back, punching his pillow into shape with a fist.

3

She had not felt the baby kick, yet. Perhaps she never would, Kit thought, when he came round from his faint, and remembered what had happened.

He saw when he looked at his watch that he had been out for no more than a few minutes. He felt cold, and nauseous. He was sick a little bit, on the ground. His hair, clothes and hands were sticky all over with Coca-Cola; where he had been lying on the ground dirt and grit were glued to the sugar so he looked as if he had been tarred and feathered.

He knew with a leaden certainty that Karim was not coming back. He, Kit, was going to get up and save Alice himself. This thought galvanised him, and he rose to his feet, brushing his palms on his trousers and lifting his eyes to the horizon far above him, resolved to climb out of the valley and get help.

If he could get to the road another car would pass and he could flag it down and ask for help. He should have done this before. Why had he not? And left Karim here with Alice? That would have been the right thing to do.

He went back to the car and listened for Alice's breathing, but he didn't get in. He didn't want her to wake up before he got back. He felt a strange kind of dull anger towards her for being unconscious. He turned away from the wrecked car and without looking up again at the steepness of the slope above him, began to climb.

Using his hands for balance, he trod, as Karim had, in minute steps up the hillside. He slipped and slid down almost as much as he climbed up, but not quite; gradually he made the ascent. His sneakers had a little bit more grip than Karim's loafers and the climb was not quite so hard. Each step required him to jam the edge of his shoe into the loose surface, to pin his fingertips into the ground. Then he could shift upwards, six inches at a time.

To his dismay a tune drifted into his mind and began to circle in his brain, repeating itself over and over until he thought it would drive him demented: *Ta-ta-ta-ta, ta-ran-ta-ra...* It was from a musical, something he had sung as a child, something cheerful and inappropriate... Oh God, he would go mad (*Ta-ta-ta-ta, ta-ran-ta-ra*) if he had to endure this fresh torture. He almost wept again, at the injustice of it all. Sweat trickled into his eyes, his dry mouth clacked open and shut as he breathed and the tune buzzed round his head like a lazy wasp and would not be dislodged.

Every few yards Kit checked his phone to see if it was receiving a signal, but there was nothing. He wasn't surprised because steep hills surrounded him on every side, turning brown and purple as the light faded. The landscape looked like velvet, one hill blurring against another, until it was impossible to distinguish between them and it seemed as if he were climbing up the inside of a dark bowl, towards its lip, with the sky a bright piece of sheet metal above.

What had taken the car a few seconds to descend took Kit an hour at least to climb. He fell several times, losing his grip, sliding downwards at speed and having to throw himself flat against the slope to stop his descent. It wasn't long before his fingertips hurt from trying to get a purchase on the stony ground, his back ached from climbing in the all-fours position, his head thumped and his mouth tasted clotted and stinking, as if he'd been sick several days before and not yet cleaned his teeth.

It was with a feeling of triumphant relief that he at last rolled on to the road and lay there panting on his back, pushing his sweaty hair out of his eyes and letting all his muscles relax for a moment. *If only I could lie here for the rest of the night*, he thought, looking up at the glittering sky.

But it was cold, and now it was dark, and only the wind playing through the hills made any sound at all. Making a colossal effort of will, Kit stood up and pulled his telephone from his pocket, looking at the screen for the thousandth time. No bars.

He was not surprised; he was resigned to the worst case scenario. It had been obvious since he had regained consciousness on the valley floor that there would be no easy path out of this situation. He had decided he would walk for help and walk he would, as far as he had to. He imagined returning to the Mercedes, taking Alice's hand as she emerged from the car, holding it as they travelled in an ambulance to hospital. He imagined her opening her eyes and whispering, 'Kit'.

He knelt beside the road and with his sore fingertips dragged together a pile of stones so that he could recognise the spot when he came back with help, and then he set off back the way they had come in the car. His shirt clung to his back and then the sweat dried on him and he felt the chill of the night air. He kept to the inside of the road to avoid slipping off the edge and tumbling back into the valley. He trudged along for a mile, and then for five miles; for an hour, and then for two.

4

For some reason the Peace Hotel at Wadi Musa had thought that they were honeymooners. On their bed was a scattering of petals and a card: 'Welcome, Mr and Mrs Miller'. Alice thought this was very funny, Kit less so.

As newlyweds they were entitled to a complimentary massage, according to the card, and to an enormous fruit basket which was delivered as they unpacked. Kit was about to say, 'Do you think anyone ever actually eats the fruit from one of those things?', when Alice plucked an apricot from the top of the pile and bit into it. So instead Kit heard himself say, 'Don't you think you ought to wash that first?'

'What? Oh, no, you don't want to worry about that sort of thing,' she replied airily. She wandered around the room, looking in all the drawers and cupboards. 'This is a funny sort of hotel, isn't it?'

Kit was tired. He stopped unpacking and straightened up. 'Funny how?'

'It feels like it's only just opened. All this furniture… it looks like it was just moved in here today.'

With exaggerated patience, Kit looked around the room. 'I don't know what you're talking about,' he said.

Alice was quiet, and ate her apricot. Then she said, 'I think we should have dinner and get an early night, don't you?'

Kit thought that real life lay outside the hotel's revolving door and not in its buffet restaurant, where tourists shuffled in patient queues. But Karim, the driver who had met them at the airport, shook his head when they asked him to recommend somewhere to eat in the town. 'No,' he said, 'this place is not good for you. The hotel is better. It is five star.'

They dismissed him and set out on foot but his words seemed to hang above them wherever they went and to pollute the air. It seemed different now from the living place they had seen through the car windows. They had driven past bustling restaurants filled with families; now those restaurants had become empty rooms, lit a cold blue by strip lights and guarded by men clustered at pavement tables. As Kit and Alice walked past, hand in hand, they felt scrutinised.

They could not decide where to settle and wandered around, up hills and down winding streets, until both were tired and irritable.

'Fuck,' said Alice, 'I've *got* to eat.'

'I've got to have a drink,' replied Kit. He was bored of Alice being pregnant, her demands more deserving than his.

After a pause Alice turned to him, 'Oh *God*, shall we just go back to the hotel? I'm getting fed up.'

'All right, if you want to. 'But it seems a bit pathetic. I mean, they're all tourists in there, eating pizza.'

'*We're* tourists, and I bet there's other food too, there's got to be. I bet you can get houmous and falafel and stuff.'

'Well then, we should have gone there in the first place,' said Kit.

'Oh, Kit, don't be so narky,' cried Alice, letting go of his hand.

'Stay here a second,' said Kit, 'I want to buy a pack of cigarettes.' He left her there and crossed the road, ducking into a shop without turning round.

It had dawned on him that they did not know how to behave with each other; the territory was unfamiliar. Although they had been away together once before, to Los Angeles, it had been Kit's trip. He had had an exhibition and Alice had accompanied him. They had stayed with Kit's American dealer, Josh, in Santa Monica, and been so well looked after that it was not much like going abroad – certainly not like the travelling that Alice had done before she met Kit. Josh flew them business class and he provided a car for Alice to use during the day when he and Kit were busy hanging the exhibition. Alice had been expected to loaf, shop, and to swim in the pool. In fact she had taken Josh's dogs into the hills above Malibu to walk – or hike, as they called it there. In the evenings she, Josh and Kit would all go out for dinner to meet up with Josh's friends, most of whom had known Kit for years.

One morning after one of these dinners, Kit had said to Josh, on the way to the gallery in the car, 'Why do we go out with these young girls, Josh? We know it doesn't work.'

Josh laughed. 'Because we love fucking them,' he said. It was a typical Josh answer.

'But sometimes…' Kit began, and then did not finish.

'Yeah, there's a downside,' Josh said. 'They don't participate. But Alice is great,' he continued. 'She's got opinions; she's got character.'

'She needs some direction,' replied Kit, restless, flicking the air-conditioning to 'off'.

Josh laughed. 'You say that, and then she'll get a career, and you'll get all jealous and needy. Isn't that what happens?'

But that's not what happened this time. One morning Alice had rung Kit and asked him to come and meet her in Holland Park. Her voice was so hollow he thought she had found him out about something, and he almost didn't go. But then he had caught sight of her suede boots lying splayed on the bathroom floor, and had thought of her legs in them. He had gone to meet her after all, and she had told him she was pregnant.

After that his life had ceased to be his own. *Baby has rights*, Rob had warned him in the pub one evening soon after, and now Kit knew exactly what he meant. Alice had moved in: those boots lived in the cupboard; her hairbrush, clogged with hair, on the hall table; her car in the space in front of the house. 'Can't you park on the road?' Kit said. 'The car's practically in the kitchen.'

'I don't have a permit,' said Alice, who was eating a yoghurt out of the pot and dangling her legs over the end of the sofa.

He had got used to some things and not to others. He liked her being there in the evenings, but not in the mornings. He liked the *idea* of her being there, but when he got home and she was there, he felt a flutter of panic. He began to resent taking her to restaurants when she ate so much and then was sick in the mornings. 'I'm not that hungry,' he would say, standing behind her and squeezing her around the waist. 'You could make something here, couldn't you?' He liked clean sheets on the bed, a dry bathmat, and his socks bound in neat pairs in the sock drawer. He did not like the fact that someone knew his habits; that he was predictable, and under observation.

In the cigarette shop the radio was on very loud, but not quite tuned to a station. The sound roared: static interspersed with shouting. Kit had come in here to avoid snapping at Alice, and now he stood in front of a fridge full of Coke cans and took a few deep breaths. It was not her fault; they were both tired; they needed to eat. He asked for a packet of Marlboro, handed over some notes and ran back across the road to Alice. She looked pitiful, standing alone on the kerb with one hand resting on her tummy.

'Come on, you're right, let's go back to the hotel,' he said, and wrapped his arm around her. But she was furious at having been left alone on the pavement, and refused to collude with him and be more cheerful. She wasn't hungry, she said, it was too late. She felt sick. She wanted to go to bed. If he was going to smoke could he do it somewhere far away from her.

Kit said he would smoke in the bar and come to bed in a minute, which he did, after a few beers and some sorrowful thoughts about his situation and his future. When he arrived back at the room she had turned off all the lights and so he woke her as he stumbled about. It was not quite what he had envisaged when he had booked the holiday, he thought to himself as he slid under the sheet next to her, holding his breath because of the beer and tobacco fumes, dreading the gritty sheet at the toe-end of the bed. Alice gave a loud snore. He turned on his side to face away from her, and exhaled a long breath.

5

Placing one foot in front of the other (as he had been doing for the last few hours and, as it felt, for most of his life) had become so automatic that when head-lights rounded a corner ahead of him and blazed in his face Kit couldn't think what was happening for a moment and stood stupefied. Then he stepped into the middle of the road, waving his arms like a clockwork toy. He had rehearsed this moment in his head and here it was, he did know what to do, this was what. He supposed he had almost been asleep while walking.

But still, when the car did pull up in front of him and he knew it was the moment of rescue, his legs turned to putty and he nearly slipped to the ground. He had to place both hands on the bonnet of the car to support himself, and take fluttering breaths, making an 'O' of his mouth. He heard the car's passenger door open and suddenly Karim – Karim! – was beside him, holding his shoulders and saying, 'Sir, sir, it's Karim. Sir, sir...' Now

Kit was trembling all over, and couldn't speak. Another man came and held him on his feet, and Kit's ears were filled with the sound of the car's engine and that of another vehicle, a pick-up truck, which waited behind it. Chattering with self-importance, Karim helped Kit into the back seat of the car and sat beside him as they drove back along the road the way Kit had come.

They swept past the pile of stones and Kit waved his arms at it and tried to tell them to stop the car, but Karim shushed him, 'Yes, yes, don't worry', and made reassuring sounds. And sure enough, after another few miles of gradual descent on the road, they were able to take a right-handed turn off it and bump downhill still further, and then turn right again and start to approach from beneath the place where the car lay.

In front the dirt was illuminated white by the headlights and small bushes appeared like skeletons before being crushed beneath the wheels. When their route became too steep and twisting, Karim, the driver and Kit abandoned their car and climbed into the pick-up behind, which was driven by an elderly man who stared gloomily ahead as if he were stuck in rush-hour traffic.

The pick-up bumped along at a walking pace, climbing, twisting, forced to slow to a crawl to negotiate boulders and more substantial bushes. Once or twice Karim and the other fellow climbed out and pushed smaller rocks out of the way so that immovable ones could be got around. For Kit the journey was an agony. He tried to calculate how long it would take but he was so confused by the dark, and by their route, that he gave up. It seemed an untold epoch ago that they had sped past his pile of stones on the road. How many more hours could they take to get back to the place which lay directly below it?

Karim must have been wondering the same thing since he soon began to bicker with the driver, gesturing in front and rubbing at the windscreen. The truck ground to a halt and stuttered in its place while the three men argued over Kit's head. Just as Kit was about to scream with frustration, trapped in between them with the gearstick shuddering next to his thigh, the driver executed a nine-point turn and crept backwards for a few hundred yards, and then even more slowly up a narrow path to one side, his wheels astride it.

After several long minutes more of crawling uphill, all four men clinging on to the dashboard, and the pick-up's owner shaking his head as rocks went clunk underneath or screeched against the side panels of the truck, the front wheels heaved over a broken lip of dried mud and they emerged in a flat space, about fifteen yards across, and steep-sloped on all sides. It was the Coke can lying on the ground that alerted Kit, and then his heart was set pounding by the black shape, the despised black shape, of the upside-down Mercedes.

The low-level argument in the car became a torrent of high-pitched chatter. Karim flung open the door and leapt from his seat, triumphant. He ran towards the Mercedes, followed by his friend. The driver of the pick-up and Kit, whose legs seemed to have stopped receiving instructions, sat together for a moment with the engine idling and the passenger door standing open. Kit became aware, for the first time, of the radio playing. He and the lugubrious man beside him watched the other two run forward, illuminated by the headlights, and then Kit noticed that the front door of the Mercedes was no longer propped open as he had left it. The water bottles he had used as door stops lay on the ground beside the vehicle. Kit felt his hair lift from his head in apprehension as he computed this information, and it was with no surprise, therefore, that he watched Karim pull open the car door, poke his head and upper body inside, and then emerge and turn back to face them, mute, but with a question mark in his expression.

6

In the morning they had discovered each other in the bed and made love underneath the hotel counterpane, whispering and not quite awake. As was usual, sex had acted like a blessing on their mood and, full of energy, they sprang from shower to breakfast where they sat united, mocking the other guests. They then collected cameras and water bottles from their room and set out to explore Petra before it became too hot. Alice wore a complex web of long-sleeved and long-legged garments in order to keep the sun off, topped by a broad-brimmed cotton hat and sunglasses. 'Sorry about this,' she said. 'I know it's not very sexy but I don't want the baby cooking all day like a little baked potato.'

They walked down the hill through Wadi Musa, hand in hand until they both became too sweaty. Kit declared the place a 'dump', and was pleased when Alice agreed. Last night she had been picky and defensive, but today they were in accord. The town seemed to exist, Kit went on, purely for the purpose of serving the charabancs of tourists who came to look at Petra. It had no heart.

They hurried down the dusty road, past a row of five-star hotels, and into the mayhem of the site complex itself. People were everywhere, standing in the dust in self-conscious groups, looking around with expressions both docile and expectant. Everyone seemed to be waiting for a person of authority to tell them what to do. *We are not like you*, Kit thought in panic. He held Alice's hand with a kind of defiance.

Their satisfaction with each other made them light-headed, batting away children who asked for money, and men who offered their services as guides. Kit had a guide-book; he did not want a guide in person. 'They'll only try to tell me about Indiana Jones,' he said. They paid their money and wandered down the path into the canyon. 'This is called the *siq*,' he told her, looking up from the page. Alice was staring up at the slit of blue sky visible between the pink walls.

'Extraordinary,' she murmured. 'You could look and look, and never know.'

'Yes, that's what happened,' said Kit. 'There were rumours of an ancient Nabatean city... but no one knew exactly where.'

But when he looked up again, Alice had wandered on.

It was strange, but despite the hundreds of people that thronged the entrance, because of the twists and turns of the canyon walls, it became possible to feel as if they were practically alone. Groups of guided tourists were led past them and away around corners, and Kit and Alice would be left in the almost-quiet, almost-cool shade of the chasm. Alice was fascinated by the fig trees that sprang from cracks in the cliff walls. 'How can they live?' she said. 'They've nothing to cling to.'

Kit began to be irritated by what she noticed, and what she ignored. 'Look, this is a gutter,' she said at one point, putting a hand into a neat, smooth drain that ran at hip-height alongside their path.

'Yes,' said Kit, 'this was the way the water came in. They had a sophisticated drainage system. Or perhaps that was the Romans?' He frowned and turned the pages of his book.

Alice was distracted by the horses that clattered up and down, pulling carriages. 'The poor things. I can't look.'

'Well then, don't,' replied Kit, too hot for sentiment.

At one point he saw her taking photographs of the ground. He went and stood beside her. 'So funny,' she said. 'The guides must all stop and have their fag break here. Look – '

Kit looked down at the ground and saw a small heap of cigarette butts tucked into the crevice of an ancient carving.

He felt a surge of discontent and said, 'You do find the oddest things interesting.'

Alice turned the camera towards him and snapped his picture. Then she looked at the portrait on the screen. 'Sourpuss,' she said. Kit felt a flash of temper.

They continued winding through the *siq* and finally glimpsed the Treasury, *Al Khazneh*, in front of them. 'Holy cow,' said Alice, walking on with her mouth open. 'That is amazing.' They rounded the final corner and stood in the open, confronted by the façade. '*Amazing*,' she said again.

Kit was bothered by the crowds. 'Perhaps if we climb up one of these paths. We can get away from some of these people.'

But Alice wasn't listening. 'Look,' she said, 'there's a café, thank God. I can sit down and have a cup of tea.'

7

She had wandered into the desert, and Kit could not, when they found her and woke her up, bring himself to ask her why. Now she was being examined by doctors, and he waited with Karim outside the surgery door, the two of them next to each other on scuffed plastic chairs. Sometimes Kit held his head in his hands. Anxious and silent, Karim watched him, or stared at the ceiling. At one point they both went outside and smoked a cigarette, and Kit noticed that daylight had broken the dawn, and the next day had begun.

When Karim handed Kit the lighter Kit saw that his fingertips were bloodied and the nails torn, from crawling up the side of the valley. Kit remembered how he had not believed Karim would come back, and was ashamed. He looked at his own hands and found similar marks.

If he had stayed with Alice, he thought, she would not have left the car, and time would have been saved, time when he and the three other men had had to fan out into the darkness, only two of them carrying torches, to try and find her. The blackness had been horrifying to Kit then. They could not use the headlights of the truck because they had come by the one passable route. They would find her on foot or, when it was light, with a helicopter, but Kit was not at all sure she would be alive if they found her in the morning. They had called and shouted, 'Alice! Alice!' but nothing had come back except echoes off the rocks and the dense buffet of the wind. At one point Kit had stopped and squatted on his heels in the dirt to weep and beg, rubbing his eyes with his fists, and it was then that the driver of the truck had shouted something, and Karim had called back to him with a whoop in his voice, and Kit had known that Alice had been found.

There was no seat for them on any flight out of Amman that day, and nor was there a room for them at the Peace Hotel in Wadi Musa where they had stayed before the accident. In the lobby Alice sat on a cane chair and drank one glass of mint tea after another. Kit stood beside her with the hotel's Malaysian manager, Mr Lim, and tried to decide what they should do. Mr Lim clasped and unclasped his hands. He had worked at this hotel for six months. Before that he had managed one in Kuala Lumpur, owned by the same chain.

In the end they agreed – or rather, Mr Lim suggested, Kit concurred and Alice nodded – that they continue as planned: drive to the Dead Sea and stay at the hotel into which they were still booked for one remaining night, and then fly out of Amman in the morning. There seemed to be no better idea. Kit thought Alice might not want to do that drive again, but Mr Lim knew another route – longer, but straighter – which avoided the scene of the accident, and so it was decided.

Kit didn't want to keep asking her if she was sure she felt all right. He could not quite believe the two doctors, both of whom had said that she and the baby were fine. It was a boy, they knew now, just as she'd always said it was. 'Tough little chap,' Kit said with pride, squeezing Alice's hand. Nobody seemed as worried as he was – he supposed that in a place like this babies survived far worse ordeals. Alice seemed to think that she would know if there were something wrong, and Kit felt unqualified to disagree out loud, at least in present company. She said she was tired and hungry, and wanted a bath. Mr Lim ordered breakfast for her – Kit was fascinated to hear him speak fluent Arabic, as well as English – and she ate pitta with olive oil and halloumi while the two men stood and discussed the journey over her head.

Bent double with sympathy, Mr Lim shook hands with them both and placed them in the care of his personal driver, who pursed his lips and spoke not a word for the entire journey. Both his hands remained on the steering wheel; his telephone lay untouched in his shirt pocket; he did not adjust the temperature. Kit, seatbelted into the back with Alice, felt grateful for this attention.

Kit had tried to give Karim some money before they parted but he would not take it. Karim had to go and report the accident to the police, but Mr Lim said the police would not need to see Kit and Alice unless they were pressing charges. 'Of course not,' said Kit, loud and clear. 'It was an accident.'

He shook hands with Karim and Alice did too. Karim took her hand in both his own and bent his head towards the ground. Kit felt sad and sorry for him, and wondered whether he would lose his job.

Kit tried several times, at the start of their car journey, to hold on to Alice's hand, but like a little minnow it kept slipping from his grasp. He looked sideways at her across the back seat of the car. He had thought she'd gone to sleep but she was staring out of the window. He watched her for a moment, willing her to turn and face him, but she did not.

8

On the barren, sloping eastern shore of the Dead Sea loomed their hotel, a vast edifice built of yellow stone. It was brand new and looked as if it had been dropped, fully furnished, from the sky. Instead of lying in the landscape, it seemed to sit high on its foundations like a sandcastle, looking as if a wind or a tide might wipe it away. Beneath the building, in the gaze of its hundreds of dark-tinted glass windows, neatly terraced gardens led down to the seashore. Tall palms and gnarled olives looked quite natural, springing from their beds, but Kit realised as he gaped at the view from reception that the trees – every single plant, in fact – must have been imported, and bedded in imported soil. More amazing still was the water which poured, gushed and burst forth in fountains all over the artificial garden. Artful rock formations made it look as if springs erupted from the ground and yet in every direction beyond the walls of the complex there was nothing but sand and salt water.

Uniformed staff with glassy smiles slid across the shining lobby floor carrying loaded trays and piles of folded towels. There seemed to be no other guests. 'Where is everybody?' Kit asked the concierge. He was told that there was a conference taking place at the hotel, and all its guests were on a day trip to Aqaba. They would be back later for dinner in 'Refresh', the hotel's buffet restaurant.

Kit and Alice were taken by golf buggy to their room which was in a sand-coloured villa, separate from the main building. It was air-conditioned to a numbing chill and Kit, irritated, asked the bellhop to help him change the temperature. 'I don't know why you people think it's a luxury to sit in a fucking fridge,' he snapped when Alice was out of earshot, knowing the boy could say nothing in response. Then, ashamed of himself, he searched in his pockets for a tip. As he handed it over he felt weary and homesick.

Alice had opened the balcony doors, inviting a flood of warm, damp air into the room. She had stepped outside and Kit joined her there. Together they watched a huge yellow sun struggle through thick grey air towards the western horizon, an outline of white bare hills above the sea. He supposed that was Israel. A skein of white birds traced a scribble across the sky, high above them, flying east. Beneath their balcony the hotel garden was deserted. It felt as if there had been an emergency evacuation.

The clotted atmosphere and the ingenious fakery of the place gave Kit a feeling of immeasurable dread. It felt like a place designed by a non-human species, where experiments were carried out on captured humans made docile by their surroundings. It was luxury – 'five star' as Karim had kept repeating proudly – but not to Kit. His skin crept with anxiety, and he longed to go home. He sought Alice's hand with his and rubbed her palm with his thumb as she liked him to do, but Alice was unresponsive and the dread clutched him ever tighter. The sea below lay still and unruffled, its surface unreflecting, a dull pigeon grey.

'What should we do?' he asked.

'Swim,' said Alice. 'We should swim. In the sea. That's what people come here for. And we don't have long before the sun sets.'

They dug their swimming clothes out of their luggage and wandered through the gardens towards the water. Golden sand had been laid along the shore and furnished with sun loungers, folded towels and colourful umbrellas, whipped by a coarse wind. A smiling man stepped forward to accommodate them; there was no one else there.

Kit ordered drinks which he knew would never be brought. He stood looking at the water with no enthusiasm. Scenting a possible reprieve, he turned to Alice. 'Are you sure you should?' he asked. 'Swim, I mean?'

'Yes, why not?' she said in surprise. 'It's only salt water. And I don't have to swim – I'll float. I can't wait.' She looked at him, shading her eyes. 'Don't you want to?'

'Yes, of course I do.'

They inched down to the water together, and Kit helped Alice down some concrete steps, encrusted with a milky layer of salt deposit, and into the water. 'Oh!' she said in surprise. 'It's freezing! I thought it would be hot. How funny.'

'It's not freezing,' mimicked Kit. 'It's not even cold.'

'It feels cold to me,' said Alice, her tone mild.

The smiling man appeared behind them and said, 'You must be careful – no splashing.' He pretended to rub his eyes with his fists. 'Very painful.'

'Oh yes,' said Kit, 'I hadn't thought about that.' He dipped his hand into the water and tasted it. 'It's like a gargle.'

Alice was tiptoeing forward over the stones and Kit followed her. He was disappointed. He had wanted the water to taste, look or feel different – be somehow more dense – but it seemed no different from the ordinary sea. But then, as he walked further in, he felt the water uproot him. He found himself floating on his back, and so was Alice, and neither of them knew quite how. Alice's face – surprised – smiled at his expression, which he supposed was the same. The spell that had held him in a frown all day was broken. He exhaled. The previous day and night receded.

But the wind came, ruffling the water from the west, and little waves came with it. Kit started to be anxious about splashing his eyes. He floated for a few minutes and then the novelty wore off. He stood up and looked towards the artificial beach. The hotel was a strange kind of oasis, decked in yellow and green, and the rest of the shore stretching away on either side was barren, a mess of brown stones. Kit felt chilled. Alice had been right: it was cold. Taking great care not to make a splash, he lay back in the water again and paddled himself back to the concrete steps. He climbed out of the water and on to the sand where the smiling man handed him a towel.

'Are you all right in there?' Kit called to Alice.

'Heaven,' she said, and she did look comfortable,

floating on her back with her head out of the water and her eyes shut.

Back in the room Kit stood under the shower for a long time, feet apart, hands placed on either wall of the shower, head bent and water streaming off his chin. Then he scrubbed every part of his body with the complimentary loofah and Dead Sea Salt Scrub he found on the wire rack. He covered himself in a lather, washed his hair and rubbed his scalp with his fingertips. He tipped his head on one side, then the other, and let the water thunder into each ear. He got out of the shower and shaved, examining every part of his face as if he hadn't seen it for a long time. He combed his hair, brushed his teeth, wrapped a towel around his waist and came back out of the bathroom feeling very hungry.

He could see Alice, sitting in a wooden armchair on the balcony, her form indistinct in a white hotel dressing gown. He watched her for a moment. He could see her lips moving and her hands stroking her belly. She was talking to the baby.

Joining her, he interrupted, saying, 'Come on, you should eat, shouldn't you? Let's get dinner out of the way and then we can go to bed. You must be exhausted.'

'I am,' said Alice. 'Help me up, would you?' She stretched up her arms and he took her hands and helped her to stand. Upright, she smiled at him and, still holding his hands, leaned forward and turned her face to rest on his chest. He wrapped his arms around her and felt hers go round his waist.

It's going to be all right, he thought. Thank God. It was the first time he had held her since the accident. Other people had handled her – the driver of the pick-up, the doctor, Karim – but not him. 'Should we talk about what happened?' he asked.

'Ugh,' she said, her voice muffled, 'Not tonight. Let's wait; be quiet together. It's all so…' she tailed off.

'I can't wait to wake up to another day.'

'I know exactly what you mean.'

They kissed, and then dressed, in perfect mutual understanding. Kit's relief was immense, and as they made their way to the restaurant he felt less cautious of her. The accident had been lodged between them all day like a bolster, but now they were clasped together again.

Outside the room it was dark. Hand in hand, they made their way along winding paths, overhung by palm fronds, to the main hotel building. As they walked past other villas they heard showers running, voices, televisions, music. Kit felt reassured – there were other people here! Doing normal things! – and he smiled at another couple, also hand in hand, who stood to one side to let him and Alice pass.

In the hotel lobby they took the lift to the top floor and stepped between its doors into the restaurant: a large, circular room, a section of which opened out on to a terrace. They sat at a table and both looked out towards the sea. Below them the fronds of the imported palms were stirred by the wind. There were no lights beyond the hotel compound – nothing on the water, nor on the opposite shore. The darkness gave Kit a rumble of fear, and he felt confidence and comfort desert him once again.

Inside, the restaurant had been painted with a mural that reminded Kit of a children's television programme: bright rainbow colours and a mural of whales, fishes and crustaceans. Music of the spangled, Indian-sounding kind beloved by hotel restaurants all over the world was being piped through speakers both inside and out. A Philippine waitress took their drinks order and then gestured towards the buffet, advising them to help themselves. Having just sat down and had their napkins spread on their knees, they got to their feet and stumbled towards the food.

A sort of madness overtook Kit at the buffet. He supposed he was too tired to make sensible choices. He hovered at the various food stations, using tongs to place one thing or another on his plate, handling each piece of food with great care, as if it were made of glass. The muzak seemed to swell in his ears, an orchestrated version of a pop anthem played here by a thousand violins, all reaching a mighty crescendo as he stood examining a tray of chicken drumsticks basted in a cold white mayonnaise.

He could see Alice laughing with the chefs at the hot-food station. A chicken kebab was being turned for her on a barbecue. Kit flushed with jealousy: he was alone; anxiety squeezed his head; he was swamped by self-pity. He looked down at his plate and saw a spoonful of pasta salad, a boiled potato and some chopped egg. He was useless. He had not rescued Alice; he had made things worse. He had abandoned her; he had lost her. He wanted to hurl his plate into the sky, egg and potato notwithstanding, and then to vault off the terrace after it.

When he woke in the night his head swam with confusion and he felt as if he were surfacing from deep under water. It was very cold – the air-conditioning must have sprung to life again. The sheets had all gone from the bed. It was dark. Where was Alice? He could hear water, pouring, somewhere, but could not think what was going on. He reached for a light switch and pressed a button on the panel at random. At once the room was ablaze – he had lit all the lights with one touch – as if it were on stage. He stared around him and shrank in horror on the bed, all his senses clanging at once in terrified alarm.

There was blood everywhere. He, and the bed, and the bedclothes on the floor, were soaked in it and all the way to the bathroom there were smudges and footprints. 'Oh my God, oh my God. Alice!' Kit said, not in a shout but in a whisper, jumping up, tripping, stubbing his toe on the coffee table, stumbling, rushing into the bathroom, skidding on the wet floor.

She was sitting in the corner of the shower with her knees drawn up, her head against the wall and her eyes shut. Wet hair was plastered against her head and water rained down around her. But flooding out of the shower where she had not shut the door came a red tide, blood and water mixed, all over the floor, sopping into the towels and circling down the drain, and Kit saw that blood was pouring out of her as if she were a vase, carelessly knocked over on a table.

Part Two

1

Shrinking from the cold of the early morning, Alice stood on Wormwood Scrubs, her gloved hands deep in her coat pockets, her hat pulled down to her eyebrows and her chin buried in her scarf. The wind was making her eyes water. She put her back to it and waited with hunched shoulders for her dog to catch her up. Wormwood Scrubs, as bleak and gloomy a place as its name suggests, had not yet noticed the coming of the spring, or indeed of the day: it was as dark and cheerless as at the dawn of a Siberian winter.

A grass plateau, muddied in places, was laid out in front of her and pierced by football and rugby goalposts which stood stark against the white-bound sky. The northern fringe, where the common was bordered by a brown plait of railway lines, contained an avenue of young, elegant trees, none of which seemed to contain the energy or the optimism to bring themselves into leaf. On its southern side the green plain was walled in by gloomy blocks and towers: the hospital and the prison. Here and there in the grass were dotted clumps of dank-looking shrubs, the dark soil beneath them shingled with beer cans, bottles and fistfuls of toilet paper.

Isolation; desolation; bleakness; abandonment – it was no wonder she felt so at home here. She had tried to walk in Kensington Gardens, but it seemed always to be full of children, whichever route or time of day she chose. Babies pushed in buggies came rolling towards her, and she had so little time to prepare herself. What could she do, turn away? No, she had to continue, with her eyes averted, as if she had a phobia. Sometimes she went there at the very end of the day, wandering in the gloom until the gates were locked, but children seemed to leave their mark – like handprints on a glass window, or warm breath on a cold morning – and she was haunted.

Here on the Scrubs she could walk the perimeter and not encounter a soul. She had used to come later in the morning but then she ran the risk of being approached by other walkers, women in waxed mackintosh coats and wellington boots who had dropped their children off at school and now strode across the windswept turf with proprietary airs. Since Alice now woke up in what Kit called 'the middle of the fucking night', she might as well be here as wide-eyed in bed, staring at the ceiling, waiting for the street lights to switch off.

Bones, the elderly and fastidious yellow dog that accompanied her, was as antisocial as she was. If they met another dog walking with its owner, she would greet it with the physical picture of Alice's feelings: a kind of frozen horror. She would raise her ears, and then one foot, and stand quite still. If the dog bustled towards her, she would remain motionless, stiff with antipathy. Most other dogs would be defeated by her force of will alone and would drift off-course and glance at her sideways from a safe distance, sniffing a tuft of grass. Sometimes they still tried to address her and she tiptoed round them, looking disgusted. Alice felt she and Bones had a mutual under-standing.

Alice waited. Bones sniffed at a clump of long grass and then, taking two steps forward with her usual cer-emony, squatted over it while looking off into the dis-tance. Turning back into the wind, Alice bent her head and walked on.

At the furthest reach of the common she found a place where someone had lit a bonfire the night before. A porridge of ash and dirt lay in place of the grass, and beer cans had been thrown into the embers. Tramps, Al-ice thought, not kids. Kids left the burned carcasses of scooters, and empty bottles of ready-mixed cocktails. Tramps made neat fires – camp fires – and sat around them with cans of beer. She stared at the ground and felt hollow with gloom. *I am so much better off than so many people*, she thought. *Why can't I feel it?* After a few moments she looked up and turned back towards home, the wind cutting across her jaw like a cold blade. Placing one foot before the other with purpose, but with-out interest, she made her way back to her car.

Sitting with the engine on and the heater turned up, try-ing to get warm, she thought of the day before her. She would not go home – to Kit's house – right away. He would be up, and in the kitchen. She would go there later when he had left for work.

The purpose of her day was now twofold. First, to get as far through it as possible without being seen – by Kit or by anyone else who knew her. She could escape Kit by getting up before him and staying out until he had gone to the studio. She had used to have a job, of course, but not any more. A week after their return from Jordan, when she had thought things were going to go back to normal, she had gone to work. A week later she had stopped going, and Kit had made no comment.

After her walk on the Scrubs she would go to a café with a newspaper and drink a cup of tea. She would stay there for forty minutes or so and then she would walk to the other end of the Portobello Road and repeat the process in another café. If, on the street, she saw anyone she knew, she would duck behind a bit of street furniture until they were gone. If someone stopped her to say hello, she would pretend she had to be somewhere else and rush away from them, glancing at her watch and making gestures of apology.

After the second café she would go home, quite tired by now, and lie on the sofa with Bones draped over her like a blanket. She might turn the pages of a magazine, or switch on the television. She did not like to watch films any more because they could not hold her concentration.

The second goal she tried to meet each day was to eat as close to nothing as possible. This had become a new and consuming occupation, taking up almost as much time and energy as a job of work.

Recently she had started to be woken in the night by hunger pangs (she knew what these were now: her insides gripping and ungripping themselves, making strange, rebellious noises), or because she was soaked in sweat and chilled to the bone. She and Kit no longer shared a bed – or a bedroom – so there was no one to disturb when she got up, peeled off her sodden clothes, put on dry ones and got back in the other side to avoid the soaked pillow and sheets.

Before she fell back to sleep she was sometimes afraid of her body, the pleading noises it made and the other unnerving developments: her skin prickling as if she might shed it; worm-like currents coursing up and down her legs; the clicking of her joints when she turned over in bed and the cold ache at the base of her spine.

But she knew something now that had never occurred to her before Jordan – that her body was not her friend, and that these were all its tricks. It was untrustworthy, deceitful and greedy. She had to stay alert, to keep a watchful eye on it. It was trying to frighten her into submission, even polluting her brain when she slept and dreamed of food.

The curious thing was that she was not trying to lose weight. In fact, she regarded her reflection, if she caught it in a shop window, with some surprise. The face now had the startled, drawn expression of a long-abandoned castaway. Coming out of the shower, she looked in the mirror with detached interest, as if she were casting an eye over someone else's physique in the changing rooms at the gym. She saw a body that was all angles, that looked as if it had swallowed a geometry set. Each breastbone was a pronounced ridge on her chest; her ribcage was hooped, quite visible all round; her pelvis stuck out below her dish-shaped midsection and every tailbone was defined at the bottom of her spine when she bent to dry her legs. One day she had thought she had found a tumour on her back before realising it was a bone she had never known existed.

No, this was not about weight, or shape. It was about keeping a newly discovered part of her – something malevolent, sullen and beast-like – on a leash. She was afraid of this creature, and if it growled in the middle of the night, then so much the better, for that meant she had got it penned in where it could not cause havoc.

Before going to Petra she had tried on one of her old bikinis to see if she could get away with not buying any more. She had tucked her new breasts, swelled with pregnancy and well-being, into the bikini top and then looked in the mirror. Looking at herself she had felt a sense of appropriateness, of calm satisfaction: *this is what a woman, a mother, looks like*. 'Kit,' she had called then, down the stairs, 'you must come and look at this.' He had come and stood behind her, both of them facing the mirror.

'It's not decent,' he had said, putting his hands on her. They had ended up on the bed, the bikini on the floor.

How little she had known, then. That girl had been such a fool.

Now she allowed herself to eat something when the alternative was a dead faint. In the morning as she got up she would assess the urgency of her need for food.

Quite often, as she dressed, her hands would shake with a kind of palsy. She would chew at her lip and take a long time to do simple tasks, like tying her laces or doing up buttons. This was good this meant that the need was desperate and that if she did not eat straight away it would only be a few minutes before one eyelid would start to droop, her arms and legs would begin to tingle and she would be confused – too confused to have a conversation, had there been anyone around to have one with. So she would dress, climb the stairs to the kitchen and eat a banana, without switching on the lights. Bones would come up the stairs behind her, *click-click-click* with her claws on the floorboards, and lie down on the rug in front of the fireplace, head on paws, waiting for Alice to pick up her car keys.

The trouble with eating something was that it made her remember how hungry she was. As she got to the end of the banana she sometimes felt like crying. How she longed for another one! She had tried mashing it up but it seemed to make less of it, even if she added water. The answer was to take tiny bites and chew it very slowly, also to concentrate on each mouthful, not be distracted and wolf it down without appreciating it. If she was reading a newspaper or looking out of the window she could easily reach the last bite without having realised she was eating, and then it was too late: she had missed her chance to take pleasure in the taste, and there would be no more until tomorrow.

Having eaten the banana, she had to get out of the kitchen in case she started thinking about eating something else. The kitchen, though lovely and warm, was a dangerous place to be. If she lived in a house with servants, it had occurred to her, she would never have to go near a kitchen. Someone would have brought her a banana on a silver tray. Open-plan living made life much more difficult. Everyone was surrounded by food all the time. How did they stop themselves from eating it? She couldn't go to friends' houses now, in case she had to sit in their kitchens. If there was a plate of leftovers or an open packet of biscuits she would be unable to concentrate on anything else. How did other people manage? They must be so much more self-controlled than she. She wished she weren't such a glutton. She knew that if she ate one biscuit she would want the packet, and be just as hungry having eaten the lot. It was better to stay away.

She had used to walk from the house to the Scrubs with Bones and then around the park and back, but now it tired her out too much so she took the car. Bones had a nest of blankets in the back and was happy to snooze there after the park while Alice tramped the streets until it was safe to go back to the house.

If she wanted to torture herself further – which she did, more often than not – she would go into the health food shop and gaze at the cakes, loaves of bread and bags of nuts. These were foods that she wanted so much she could scarcely stand it, so when she left the shop empty-handed it was with a feeling of great triumph. There were other, smaller tortures: walking past the Italian café in which you could buy a slice of pizza heated up, or past the stall in the market where a French couple made crêpes. These two smells she found almost irresistible.

Almost.

At the coffee shop croissants, dusted with icing sugar and oozing almond paste, were stacked alongside *pains au chocolat,* spilling their chocolate centres, on plates beside the till. Alice felt like a dog with rabies when she saw them: maddened by thirst, too terrified to drink. 'Any pastries for you, miss?' the girl behind the counter would ask her, waving her tongs.

Alice would feel like replying, 'Do I look like the sort of person who eats pastries?' But it was winter and so her body was a secret, under her clothes. 'No, thank you,' she would say, and take her tea off to a table where she could not see the food or anyone eating it.

To get to the end of the day she would have to allow in a few small doses of food, and in the evening she would go over what she had eaten and assess her performance. If she had done well she felt a curious triumph and hugged it to herself – it was a feeling she could thrive on, almost as sustaining as if she had eaten five courses.

It was a hard-earned satisfaction but since she had failed at everything else she was determined to achieve it. She seemed unequal to the task of a relationship with Kit and unable to do her job any more, and it was all because she had not been able to look after the little Bean, tucked away inside herself, and he had died.

In the car she became aware that she had been sitting for a while, staring through the windscreen. She cursed herself: here she was, again, thinking about herself and her dead baby, *again*. What was the point? All these wasted hours spent wondering, *Where is he? Who is looking after him now?* And she would never know! He was gone.

Glancing around at Bones, sleeping and muddied on her blanket, Alice roused herself, put the car into reverse and drove out of the car park. She flicked on her indicator, turned on to North Pole Road and headed towards Ladbroke Grove, where her day would pass.

2

She had promised, in the evening, to go and see her sister, Emmy. For most of the day she wondered how she could get out of it. But she was inclined to do what Emmy told her – as she always had done – and so she found herself, at seven o'clock, driving to Clapham from Portobello as promised. Bones lay across the back seat. At the traffic lights on Beaufort Street, waiting to cross the river, Alice rehearsed what she would do when dinner was put in front of her.

She knew that Emmy would have cooked and that because Alice was not well it would be something special, something sustaining. But Alice did not want to be sustained.

She had prepared herself by eating nothing since the banana, and drinking a lot of herbal tea, which was filling in its own way. She took swigs from a bottle of fizzy water next to her on the seat – the bubbles helped her to feel full. She held in reserve a trick she had developed for occasions such as meals with other people: to look at her plate and imagine the food lying in her guts like trimmings on a butcher's block. She would pick up a few bits and pieces with her fork, rearrange them, and then she would push the plate far away where she could not see it.

This evening Emmy was making spaghetti carbonara. They had loved it as children when Emmy would cook it if their parents went out. They had used to eat it in front of the television as a treat: Pete in the armchair, Emmy on the sofa and Alice on the floor.

Pete, their brother, was the eldest. Now a mathematics professor, he lived in America and worked at a huge, brand-new university. Alice had been there once, to visit, and had sat in on one of his lectures and not understood one single word. Not one word. What she *had* understood, however, was that every female student in the room was a little bit in love with Pete. This had made her very happy, on his behalf. Pete had not noticed, of course. He was married to a sturdy American with a pony tail like a broomstick, whom he adored, and they had three little girls with identical gazes, quizzical, that said, *You're kind of funny*.

At thirty-eight, Pete was three years older than Emmy and fourteen years older than Alice. Alice had been a mistake ('Not a mistake, an *accident*, and a very happy one,' as their mother always said.) But, happy accident or not, Alice's parents had lost interest in parenting when Alice had been growing up and it was Emmy whose influence she felt most. When Emmy had moved to London,

Alice had begun spending her school holidays there too, and then their parents had emigrated to Florida to live in a waterside apartment (a move that had appalled Emmy), and now she saw them once or twice a year. Pete and 'the girls' saw them often, and sent photographs, which Emmy would examine, hunched over her computer screen wearing a disgusted expression.

'I don't know why you mind so much what they do,' Alice would say. 'You don't have to be there, after all.'

'Because it's so not *them*... It upsets me. Look at that barbecue! It's the same size as your car. They've lost it. They've turned into those Americans we used to laugh at, lost on the Tube.'

As she pulled the cork from a bottle of wine, Emmy asked, 'Have you talked to Mum?'

'Yes,' said Alice. 'She rang, oh, I can't remember when.'

'She's worried about you.'

'I know, but I told her, I'm fine. I'll be fine. I don't want her to get in a fret and come over, or anything like that.'

'No, well, I know what you mean,' said Emmy, frowning as she poured wine into two glasses and passed one to Alice. 'I agree.' She paused and then added, 'As long as you are fine?'

'Of course I am. Nearly. It takes time – that's what everyone says.' She sipped at her wine. She had to be careful: sometimes if she drank alcohol she couldn't help herself from eating.

'You can stay the night, you know,' said Emmy,

misinterpreting these fastidious sips. 'You don't need to worry about driving.'

'Oh, I know, thanks, but in the morning I've got things...' Alice tailed off. *Stay the night!* she was thinking to herself. *It's impossible.*

For one thing, she didn't sleep much any more. She hadn't since she had been pregnant. Then she had slept with the knowledge that with her body she protected her baby, curled up inside her, sleeping too. But now she lay awake, hour after hour. Sometimes she thought about food and made plans for what she might eat in the morning – not that she ever did.

If she did not take care, other thoughts would well up in her head, before she could stop them: *Where has he gone?* Her mind would stutter to a halt, stumbling over him – *him* – and she would have to shut it down, to give her brain a powercut. After hearing the blood thump in her ears, *once, twice,* she would take a shallow breath and restart her mind again, opening her eyes, hearing her hair scratch on the pillow. But it was tiring, to be vigilant like this, all the time.

Since the miscarriage Alice had created a new version of herself who got up in the morning, walked around, answered questions when she was asked them and went to bed in the evening. It was a person who existed, but nothing more than that. If she had stuck a pin in herself, as she sometimes felt like doing, she would have watched it go in, but would she have felt it? Like someone drugged, she could see what was happening, but she didn't care. Other people's thoughts and opinions seemed distant, as if spoken in another room. Even Emmy's voice didn't penetrate.

When lying in bed at night, on her back, she was most aware of the physical loss. Resting light hands on her pelvis, there was nothing underneath them: the bump was gone. It was strange, she thought, that she had not been able to believe that she was pregnant to begin with, and now that she was not, she could not believe that either.

It was as if he had never existed, that baby boy, and perhaps he had not. Did his count, as a life? Had he ever been a baby, a child, or a person? Yes: a person; her companion; her friend; her boy.

But stop! She was doing it again: thinking about him. It was better not to. Thoughts came creeping into her mind like insidious climbing plants, their tendrils reaching in through closed windows. She had to stay alert and keep them out. She didn't speak about the baby at all; it was easy not to – she could head people off; but these thoughts – indulgent, foolish – were harder to control. They would infest her, if she allowed it.

Other people either ignored what had happened or they darted at the subject in blind panic. They might say, 'You're so young! You've got plenty of time for babies.' She would have to catch her breath and think of something far away in order not to strike out. It was pointless to be angry; pointless to be anything.

From her hospital bed in Jordan she had longed to be back in London. She had assumed that once at home, with Kit, she would feel well again and be able to participate. But she did not feel as if she had ever come home, and she seemed to be getting less well, now, as time went on. This frightened her. Was she going mad? The same questions knocked at her mind until sometimes she did indeed feel she might be going demented: *Where is he? Who is looking after him?* She would be brought up short, breathless, horrified. *Where is he? Where is he?* She should be better than this by now. She was ashamed. Why could she not stop thinking about it? Why had she not put it behind her?

At least Kit left her alone. In fact, he sometimes seemed surprised to see her, as if he had forgotten she still lived in his house.

But Emmy would not be put off. She asked questions and expected answers until Alice wound down and responded in monosyllables, her voice getting quieter and quieter, a radio running out of batteries. All Alice wanted to do was watch *Friends* and be left alone.

'Can't we watch *Friends*?' she had said to Emmy in the end, exhausted and defensive.

'Yes, of course we can, in a minute,' said Emmy, rolling a cigarette, taking her time.

This was why Alice could not stay the night. She would not get away with it: Emmy would catch on. The night sweats would give her away, or else Emmy might see her without her clothes on (there was no lock on the bathroom door). And then there was the morning: would they eat breakfast together? Did Emmy have any bananas? It was unmanageable. After all, in the old days they had eaten boiled eggs and toast for breakfast, before going their separate ways to work. Had she really? *How repulsive*, she thought now. And then there

was Bones, expecting her morning walk. There was no-
where to walk round here – well, there was the common,
she supposed, but it was so complicated – where would
she park? And there weren't any rabbits for Bones to
chase, and Emmy might want to come too, if she wasn't
working, which she might not be...

'Aren't you going to eat that?' Emmy interrupted the
clamour in Alice's head.

Alice looked down at her plate, a tangle of spaghetti,
gone cold. *Worms.* She had put some lettuce leaves on top
and eaten one of them, but she could not bring herself to
eat a single one of these maggoty strands, and certainly
not the pancetta she could see lurking underneath. Emmy
was strict about carbonara – 'It's eggs, pancetta, par-
mesan and black pepper. No other nonsense – none of
this cream, onion or mushroom crap' – because she had
learned to cook in Italy, taking herself off there for a year
after leaving school, and then coming back and working
in an Italian restaurant in London. Emmy was not afraid
of hard work. She was like a pony: at her best when em-
ployed.

'No,' murmured Alice. 'Sorry. I just... not very...
haven't been feeling...'

Emmy put down her rollie, stood up, took their plates
away and threw Alice's food into the bin. 'Don't worry,'
she said. 'It doesn't matter.'

Her kindness made Alice want to cry and tell her
everything. Instead, she sat in silence and pricked at the
end of one finger with a fork.

Emmy put the dirty plates into the dishwasher and
then sat back down and relit her cigarette. 'Are you very
tired?'

'Quite,' said Alice. 'I don't know why.' She frowned. 'I don't do anything.'

'Sometimes being tired doesn't work like that. And, not eating doesn't help.'

'I do eat,' replied Alice in her 'shut door' voice. 'I eat enough.'

Emmy said nothing, and Alice was torn, at that moment, between putting her head on the table and going to sleep for a long time, perhaps a year – maybe for ever – and getting up and leaving the house, getting into her car and going to Kit's. 'I should go,' she said, and stirred her legs.

'No, wait, stay – stay and have tea. I bought dates. You love dates!'

'Oh,' Alice paused, 'OK, for half an hour. Then I must go.'

Alice sat on the sofa with Bones and Emmy brought mint tea and a box of dates. She put the tray down and then in a swift movement, standing behind the sofa, she put her arms around Alice's shoulders and hugged them, kissing the top of her head and her hair beside her ears. 'Darling Alice,' she murmured. 'You know I'd do anything, to make it better for you? If I could.' And then she was gone again, back into the kitchen, slamming the door of the dishwasher and blowing out the candles.

Alice scrunched up her face and pinched the backs of her hands until the threat of tears went away. She composed herself. To please Emmy, she decided to eat a date and picked one up, examining it from all angles. When Emmy came back into the room Alice made sure she was watching and then ate the date in tiny bites, chewing with her eyes wide open and sipping her scalding tea. She felt the sugar impact her like an injection. *Dear God*, she thought, *it's delicious*. She could have tipped the box upside down into her mouth and eaten the lot.

They watched *Friends*, an episode they had both seen before, and for Alice it was like being given a tranquilliser. She lay on her side on the sofa and let the canned laughter wash over her. When it was over Emmy wanted to watch the news, and Alice got up to go.

At the door, Emmy took her hand and said, 'It will be all right, you know.'

Alice went very still and looked down at their hands. 'When?' she asked, her voice quiet. Then she said, 'Everyone keeps telling me "These things take time", but, how long?'

'People want to help.'

'They can't. Why won't they go away? All I want is to be left alone.'

'OK. Until when?'

'Until... I don't know.' Then she said, 'Do you think I like being like this? That I'm doing it on purpose?'

'No. I think you're depressed.'

Alice laughed, without humour. 'Yes, I think I'm depressed too.' She thought she might cry so she rattled her keys and redid the buttons on her coat. 'It's all so *boring*.'

'What is?'

'All of this. I want it to stop.'

Emmy hugged her but Alice kept her arms pinned by her sides, so Emmy could not get a purchase. 'I love you,' said Emmy. 'All right?'

'Yes,' said Alice, shrinking away. She unlatched the door and took Bones out into the night.

It was cold. She trotted to her car. The street was quiet, empty, glowing a livid orange under the street lights. Alice posted Bones into the back seat and climbed into the front herself. She turned the engine on and sat there shivering, waiting for the heater to warm up. This was better: alone again; doing rather than sitting; a quiet drive home. Driving was a helpful activity, it occupied the brain and the body, but not too much. Enough to divert, to distract, but not to absorb.

Perhaps she could become a delivery driver, she thought as she shifted the gearstick. It would require very little energy, which would be ideal: enough to sit, drive and get in and out of her van every now and again. And she would be alone, and not surrounded by food. She could deliver something promising like flowers. Everyone would be pleased to see her.

To imagine a different life was enjoyable, pleasant, and an indulgence she sometimes allowed herself. It was like being asleep and having a lovely dream. As she manoeuvred the car through empty streets, she stared through the windscreen and pictured herself wearing gold jewellery and a coloured scarf, and working at a flower stall, laughing with her regular customers as she clipped the stems of roses and stripped the leaves from scented lilies. Perhaps Bones would sleep in the shop all day, or on the pavement in the sun, and in the evening they would walk home together through the park to a flat in an attic, where she lived alone.

3

While Alice was with her sister, Kit and his friend Rob were in the pub. The two men, friends for thirty years, sat in near-silence for a couple of hours and drank their way down pint after pint of Guinness.

Kit knew that Rob's wife, Naomi, would have made Rob come out to meet him. 'Don't take no for an answer,' she would have said. 'He'll say he doesn't want to meet you but you've got to *make* him.' And Rob, just back from work, would have taken his scooter helmet down off the shelf again and headed out into the freezing cold and the stationary traffic on the Shepherd's Bush roundabout.

In the pub Rob said, 'I'll be sick tomorrow if I don't eat something.'

'Crisps,' said Kit, taking his glass away from his lips for a moment.

'No,' struggled Rob, 'something proper.'

They bought a pizza and carried it home to Kit's house.

Kit opened a bottle of red wine, and they drank that, and then a can each of Strongbow. They sat in the kitchen with the lights on full blaze, and the pizza box balanced on top of the morning's post, on the table.

The house had started to look as if Alice had never existed, Rob reflected, standing in the bathroom having a pee. He could see no trace of her – only one toothbrush, Kit's, lay beside the bathroom sink. He glanced into the bedroom and saw that the duvet had been ruffled by Kit on one side, but was still smooth on the other.

But on his way back downstairs, Rob saw a pair of smallish, muddy boots by the front door, lying underneath the dog lead which hung on a hook. 'Phew,' he said as he went back into the kitchen, 'I was beginning to think you'd done away with Alice altogether. Where is she?'

'At her sister's,' said Kit, emptying the last of the Strongbow into his glass. With a sharp movement, he used his fist to flatten the can on the table. He said nothing else about Alice.

'I don't understand you men,' said Naomi, sitting up in bed, when Rob got home and reported back, later that night. 'What did you talk about? You were there for five hours, for God's sake.'

'I don't know,' replied Rob, feeling tired, and wanting to say, *Why didn't you go yourself, then*? 'Nothing. You know what Kit's like.'

'Are they together? Is she all right? That poor child. Did he seem at all upset? Do you think he's still in shock?'

'No. I don't know. I honestly don't know the answer to any of those questions.' Rob sat on the edge of the bed and pulled off his trainers.

He had not thought about it at the time but he thought about it now. His honest opinion, he decided, was that Kit was not thinking about the baby at all. But somehow he couldn't tell Naomi this.

'You're hopeless,' said his wife, lying down again.

In bed, listening to her snore, Rob thought about their children, sleeping upstairs. *Their children.* One not his, one not hers. But still, it was true to say 'their'. The elder, Charlotte, was ten – his wife's daughter from her first marriage. Their younger child, Billy, had not quite learned to walk. His son, but not his wife's: there had been a surrogate, a woman who lived in Wales. She had done it before for another couple. Naomi had stared at her in wonder: *Given a baby away. How had she done it?*

Naomi had worried that she would not love Billy in the way she loved Charlotte; Rob had worried that he would love Billy more. But it did not work like that, they had discovered: blood had nothing to do with it. Rob thought – but he had never said – that it was like hatching a duck's egg under a chicken. The chicken took no notice when one of its chicks went 'quack'.

(If he had made this observation aloud, it might have been one of those comments that he thought quite sensible, but that Naomi might never have forgiven him for. *Which one is the duck?* He could hear her voice – incredulous, despising – as she said it.)

After Rob had pushed his helmet on to his head and

pointed his scooter in the direction of Shepherd's Bush, Kit went back into the house, shut the door and leaned on it for a few moments, staring at the floorboards.

Something had gone very wrong, he knew that much, but how to fix it? He went into the sitting room, intending to switch off the lights, but instead lay down on the couch. He allowed self-pity to suffuse him. His chin rested on his chest. *It's partly the drink*, he told himself, which was comforting.

He stared at two round impressions left in the sofa cushions, where Bones and Alice had sat next to each other during the day. Bones slept, and Alice stared into space. *You see,* he thought, *she has even taken my dog.*

Bones had arrived in Kit's life by chance. She had been palmed off on a friend of his, Patrick, many years before, when Patrick had been selling Ecstasy pills in Norwich. In exchange for a bag of pills, Patrick had accepted the dog, having been convinced that she was a valuable racing greyhound. He had brought her round to Kit's house, hoping to persuade him to buy at least one of her legs as an investment, but Kit, who had used to go dog racing at Wimbledon quite often during this period of his life, identified her not as a greyhound at all but as nothing more than a common yellow lurcher whose rough coat had been clipped smooth. He also pointed out to Patrick, by now extremely embarrassed, that there was a clue to be spotted in her name: Lady Bones. Did that sound like the name of a champion greyhound?

Patrick had tried to introduce her at home as a pet – after all, his daughter had been pestering him for a dog

– but neither daughter nor girlfriend were taken with Bones. In fact, they were alarmed by her tall, skeletal frame, revolted by her long nose and depressed by her gloomy demeanour.

Kit had opened his front door one evening and found Patrick standing there with the dog on a lead. Both Patrick and the dog looked embarrassed, as if they had been paired off at a singles party. Kit had insisted, 'Absolutely not. No way.'

'What are you talking about?' replied Patrick. 'I only came for a beer.'

Inside, Kit had given Patrick a beer and the dog had tiptoed round the sitting room before heaving herself on to the sofa and going to sleep. 'That's amazing!' said Patrick, pointing his beer bottle at her. 'It's like she's come home. Look how chilled out she is! I swear she's never done that before.'

'Hm,' mumbled Kit.

'Everyone says I should dump her on the street,' continued Patrick, 'but I can't, I'm soft.'

'*I'm* not,' retorted Kit with determination. 'I'm hard as nails.'

'Come on, mate,' said Patrick. 'You've got a big house, a garden… you won't know she's here. For a day or two, while I find somewhere else.'

Of course he never came back for her.

Kit had meant to take her to a dogs' home – the vet had told him there was one in Warwickshire for lurchers – but somehow he had never quite got there. The car had had a flat tyre and taking a dog on the train was too much effort, and anyway he hated leaving London. And the funny thing was, just like Patrick said, she wasn't any trouble. She lay about on the furniture like a tatty winter coat. When he went to work he left the garden door open so she could lie outside if it was warm enough. Sometimes she came to the studio and lay on the couch. If he took her out she never needed a lead, treading a sober path along the pavement beside him. She liked sitting in the pub under the table, wearing a martyred expression when she was stepped on. In the park she stood still as children and dogs attempted to socialise with her, waiting until they lost interest and went away.

When Alice had moved in Bones – now elderly – had regarded her with politeness, if not quite enthusiasm, rather like a mother with her favourite son's new girlfriend. But since the accident they had become inseparable. Kit was irritated by it but he did not interfere. The dog made her own choice.

On the couch Kit suppurated in dark thoughts. Alice was sapping him of energy, creativity and impulse. He wanted to get out but he knew he could not, not yet. There was nothing he could do. He was trapped! She had become powerful – passive, but powerful.

Alice had always been present, she had participated: it was something he had loved about her. If she was in a room, you would know. You would not have said, after a party, 'Oh, was Alice there? I didn't see her.' But now she seemed to have dispersed, like an aspirin in water.

She was so quiet, Kit often did not know if she was in the house. He would come back from work and stand in the hall with his head cocked, listening. Silence. Then he might click open the connecting door that led downstairs to the flat in the basement, into which she had now moved. He would stand and listen until he heard some small movement or a cough, and then he would close the door again. If she was upstairs in the main part of the house – where he lived – he might walk into the kitchen and not realise right away that she was there. She sat for hours by the window, looking out, like a dog whose owner has gone to work. What should he say to her? He was at a loss. Worse than that: he was afraid of her.

She had used to clatter through the front door in a pair of wooden-soled shoes which made as much noise as a pony, on the floorboards. A rush of air had used to enter the house with her, as if she travelled with her own weather.

She had used to lie on the bed and talk to the dog in a soft, adoring voice – 'You're nothing but a silly old *pet*, aren't you?' – while she waited for Kit to get ready. He would hear her murmurings from the bathroom while he shaved. Sometimes he had thought, *I could live like this for ever.*

But now, things were not the same. Alice had become intangible; she had slipped through his fingers and got lost. It was not that he didn't love her any more, he told himself, it was that he couldn't find her.

Perhaps she would leave of her own accord. Or, he supposed, after some more time had passed, he would be able to say, *Look, it's not working,* and then she would go back to her sister, and it would be as if none of this had ever happened.

In the meantime... bed. He heaved himself out of the chair and into the kitchen.

On the kitchen table stood a glass bowl containing two goldfish. They hung suspended in the cloudy water, facing in opposite directions. It irritated Kit to see that Alice had not changed the water in days. She had used to make such a fuss about the fish.

Kit tolerated the goldfish as long as the bowl contained nothing but fish and water. He liked it to be clean and transparent, to be able to see through it from every angle. This forced asceticism made Alice unhappy: she wanted the fish to have gravel and weeds – 'Something at least to hide in' – but Kit refused to let them have so much as a dot of gravel, declaring it suburban, and threw away any toys that Alice dropped into the water. Before the accident, Kit had begun to call the fish 'Kit' and 'Alice', as a joke. Now he had stopped.

Kit paused with his hand on the light switch, watching the fish and hearing the low buzz made by the electric clock. It was an original 'Tod Miller', made in the 1970s when Kit's father had designed a bestselling range of home furnishings for a high street chain. Almost everything in the house, in fact, had been designed by Tod – right down to the fishes' bowl.

The range had recently been relaunched – this time in a range of colours – and sold even better than it had the first time around. Tod had at first complained that 'the use of colour perverted the ideals of modernism', but he had quietened down when he saw how well they were doing.

Everything in this house was original: the Formica-topped kitchen table; the steel tube-framed sofa, uphol-stered in white velvet; the Perspex desk and chair; the white suede couch – an elegant chaise longue, in fact – on which Kit had been lying; the coffee cups, glasses, cutlery, candlesticks – everything. Even the walls were hung with framed drawings by Tod, detailed sketches for sculptures he had made in the 1950s and '60s, before he had become a designer.

Kit had lived here all his life and it did not occur to him to change anything, in part because the house still belonged to his father but in the main because his father's influence extended beyond the furniture and the colour of the walls to encompass the walls themselves, the bricks and mortar, the roof and the foundations. Kit had been hard-wired to live within this aesthetic – he would no more change the interior than he would knock the house down and build another in its place. And in any case, he liked his life to be represented in this way: clean, spare, functional. He could not think of beginning again.

Kit turned off the light and left the room. He was tired. In the hall he looked at the connecting door that stood between the upper floors and the basement. He wondered when Alice would come back. If he had thought she could act a bit more normal, then he might have considered staying up and talking to her. Trying to get back in touch with her.

When it came to the loss of the baby, he could think of nothing to say. He knew it was upsetting, he knew it was awful, but he couldn't feel it. He suspected that he had never believed, in his heart of hearts, that it would happen at all. He was afraid that Alice could see through him, that she knew he was shamming and that he didn't care. If they talked, she might confront him: challenge the veracity of his feelings. And then what? He shuddered, and with these thoughts hovering round him like flies, he turned away from the communicating door.

4

It was rare for Tod, Kit's father, to come to London. If he did, he did not stay in his house, where Kit lived, because his wheelchair, amongst other things, made it too difficult. Instead, he occupied a room in a luxurious hotel off Bond Street, the same room on every visit, and he observed certain rituals – the pleasurable kind. His breakfast was brought to the room on a trolley. At lunchtime he went to a small, family-run Italian restaurant in Soho to which he had been returning ever since he had first exhibited in London at the end of the 1950s. In the evenings he invited old friends to visit and he sat with them in the hotel bar, drinking Negronis and posting salted macadamia nuts into his mouth, one by one.

It was all the more surprising, therefore, when Kit, dressing in the morning, heard the rattle of a taxi pulling up outside his house and looked out of the bedroom window to see his father's white head emerge from the back of the cab. Kit started, saying, 'Fuck!' out loud.

Then he watched, transfixed, as Damita – the nurse – helped his father on to the pavement. He could see Tod leaning heavily on his walking frame while she paid the driver.

Even from this distance, and with a pane of glass between them, Kit could sense that every fibre of his father's being was taut with rage and pain. Kit swallowed and took a small step backwards, away from the window. When Damita turned towards the house Kit ducked back into the room, ran a hand across his head in distress, and then went downstairs one step at a time. He saw, from the bare hook in the hall, that Alice was out with the dog. This relieved him a little bit, but not much.

He took a deep breath, opened the door and said, 'Dad!', but Tod was struggling up the steps, clutching Damita's arms with both hands, and did not look up. Kit could hear his father's breath come like a weightlifter's: the hiss of pain. Tod's health seemed to have deteriorated since Kit had last seen him, but physical frailty made him no less frightening; no less titanic.

Kit collected the folding wheelchair from the pavement where it had been left by the taxi driver. He carried it into the hall, shook it open and watched Tod collapse into it, settling his tall, angular frame like a rook folding itself into a nest. Tod had designed this chair himself – at least, he had taken an old design and measured a new version to fit him exactly. A bespoke wheelchair; an original 'Tod Miller'. It had a light frame, for travelling. At home he had an electric one.

When he was comfortable and had stopped gasping and biting his lip with pain, Tod looked up at Kit. 'Christopher,' he said, which always made Kit blush, though he never knew why. Tod reached out a hand and Kit took it for a moment, feeling the knotted bulbs of the arthritic joints.

'Dad, what a surprise,' said Kit, tugging his hand away. He turned to Damita and kissed her on both cheeks. 'Hello, Damita,' he said to her. 'How are you?'

He did not expect an answer. Damita was always well – she had to be. She had been Tod's nurse for many years – since he had gone to live in Ibiza – and she had never taken a day's sickness. She held Kit by the shoulders and kissed him on both cheeks, saying, 'Oh, I'm so sorry, you poor children', making clicking sounds with her tongue and smoothing his collar and his shirt front as Kit detached himself from her. She was a small but mighty woman, and Tod could not do without her. 'But God has his ways,' she continued. 'He will give you another child, when the time is right.'

Kit blushed again. 'Thank you,' he murmured, resisting a sudden urge to take Damita by the hand, sit down on the sofa with her and cry like a child. *God damn it*, he thought, *this always happens*! Whenever his father appeared he felt eight years old and as close to tears as he always had then.

'We didn't telephone to let you know we were coming,' said Tod. 'I thought Damita had, and she thought I had – one of those things.'

This, reflected Kit, was a typical Tod statement: it might sound like an apology but it felt like an accusation. He was reminded in an instant how difficult Tod made everything. The sympathy – no, the *pity* – he had felt as he had watched his father struggle up the front steps vanished.

'Never mind,' he said. 'What will you have? A cup of coffee?'

'Damita will do it,' said Tod, waving a hand, and indeed Damita was already in the kitchen, treading about the room in her rubber-soled clogs, arranging things the way Tod liked them. 'You can push me into the sitting room,' continued Tod. 'God, it's been years since I was here. You haven't changed a thing!'

Another accusation, and yet Kit knew that if he had so much as moved a picture he would have been criticised. Without a word, he pushed the wheelchair into the sitting room and parked it with Tod's back to the window. Kit stood in front of the fireplace, resting his heels on the lip of the marble surround and leaning back on to the mantelpiece. This was a favourite pose of his; he liked to lean and smoke. He reached into his shirt pocket for a cigarette as Damita brought a tray of coffee and biscuits into the room.

She had managed to find cups and saucers he did not recognise, and the biscuits, which were laid out on a plate, she had brought herself. By these actions he was reminded that this was not his house, nor were these his belongings. Everything was his father's. He supposed Damita had made the biscuits at home and brought them with her from Ibiza. No wonder Tod lived alone. Who could meet his requirements like Damita could?

He watched her pour coffee for them both and put Tod's within his reach. Then she straightened her back, smoothed her dress in front in a satisfied gesture and returned to the kitchen.

Kit watched his father try to slide a biscuit off the plate with his useless, curled-up fingers. Seeing his father wrestle with the indignity of his disabilities made Kit's heart twist with feelings he could not bear to untangle and identify. He lit his cigarette and stared out of the window.

Tod had never met Alice, but he knew what had happened in Jordan – Kit had told him, over the telephone, that their driver had crashed the car and that Alice had lost the baby. Tod had heard but not commented on the unspoken message in Kit's words: *I am not to blame.* One of the things that most irritated Tod about Kit was his perpetual need to excuse himself. 'Please may I be excused', he had said at the end of every meal. But Tod supposed he should blame himself for it, remembering Kit's mother saying to him, 'Why do you have to snap at him all the time? He's only little.'

Tod felt sorry for Kit about the baby – it was a sorry business. He was curious to meet Alice, about whom Kit had told him nothing. 'Where is Alice?' he asked Kit now. 'I want to meet her.'

Kit frowned. 'She's out... I expect she's walking the dog. How are you, Dad?' he asked carefully. 'Are you all right?'

'Of course I am,' Tod snapped. 'Did you think I'd come to tell you I was dying of cancer or something? Does a man have to have a terminal illness to want to see his son?'

No, thought Kit, with a grim inward smile, *but it helps.*

Their last meeting had not been a success. Kit had flown to Ibiza with the intention of staying a couple of nights with his father and going to the wedding of a friend, but in the event a disagreement of such ferocity had broken out within minutes of Kit's arrival from the airport that he had not got as far as unpacking his bag, driving away instead and going to stay in an hotel.

The argument had been about art, which it always was, to a greater or lesser degree. Kit had arrived at the end of a dinner party that Tod was giving, and Tod, the better or worse for wine, had introduced Kit to the assembled group as 'My son the penny portraitist'. Tod despised Kit's work and made no secret of his opinion. 'Utterly meaningless,' he had said, with one of his mirthless laughs. 'Entirely superficial. But, lucky boy, he's found people who'll pay. Only a fool would turn down their money.' A silence had fallen around the table, broken by the scrape of Kit's chair as he had got back on to his feet with a flushed face.

It was true that Kit had fallen into portraiture, entering a painting into a prestigious competition soon after graduating from art school. Whether assisted by his surname or not, he had won first prize and had thus condemned himself to making a living by painting rich people for money, for nearly two decades. It had made him wealthy in his own right, something he could have been proud of had Tod not found the fee as offensive as the paintings. 'All I want for you,' Tod would say, 'is to do something that exercises your imagination. Something free. Something you *believe* in.'

'Spoken like a rich man,' Kit would reply, but the comment stung. He knew, when he felt like being truthful with himself, that it was not about money. Each time he finished a commission he vowed that he would turn down the next, but when it came he found he could not resist. *One more*, he would think, *and then I'll start doing my own stuff*. But he never did.

'Don't patronise me! You designed cutlery, for Christ's sake,' he had said to Tod that night in Ibiza. 'You must have been desperate.'

'I'd finished being an artist – I wanted to have some fun. I'd already said everything I wanted to say.'

Kit had shaken his head, lighting a cigarette and chucking the matches on to the table. 'That's pathetic. Artists don't retire! Look at Caro, or Paolozzi. Look at Freud.'

Tod had ground his teeth at this. He hated mention of his contemporaries. 'Freud! If only he would retire,' he had scoffed. 'There are far too many of those bloody paintings and every single one looks like a display in a butcher's shop window.'

'If you were truly an artist you'd have carried on,' Kit had said, taunting him. 'You were just a designer who got lucky.'

Bang! Tod's fist had come down on to the table and all the candles had leapt out of the candlesticks. The other guests had flinched in alarm.

'My sculptures are about *life*, and *death*, and *hell*, and *pain*...' Tod had roared. 'What do your portraits say about anything?'

'Oh, God, here we go,' Kit had groaned, taking a swig of his wine. 'This is where you tell me you won the war, isn't it? How I can't possibly know anything because I've never been shot at.'

'It's a waste of time and paint,' Tod had continued. 'You might as well frame a photograph.'

'That's the point!' Kit had crowed in triumph.

Their argument, begun many years before, never developed or progressed. The two men held positions as fixed as two boxers frozen in combat on a bronze trophy. Neither could bear quite to cut the other off: Kit lived in Tod's house and there was no question of his moving out.

Did every father endure such struggles with his son? Tod felt aggrieved, chewing and swallowing his biscuit without enjoyment.

'There is a reason I'm here,' he said now, 'and I'll come to it presently. I'm sorry you've had such a bad time,' he continued, 'Of course, in our day – I mean mine and your mother's – women miscarried all the time. Now everyone seems to take it very seriously, but I expect that's a good thing.'

Kit swallowed the gust of rage that inflated his chest. Another Tod Miller classic.

'Have you spoken to Iona recently?' he asked, managing to keep his voice level.

This was a more reliable topic: he and his father were able to unite in mutual condescension of Kit's mother. They could become quite amicable when discussing her shortcomings, regarding her with a sort of pitying indulgence as if she were a lunatic, harmless but dependent, for whom (out of pure charity) they had taken responsibility.

'Yes, I have, as a matter of fact,' said Tod, clawing for

another biscuit. 'I'm going to visit her, tomorrow, for a day or two.'

This was surprising, and Kit felt disconcerted. Tod despised the country and had visited Iona twice in all the years she had lived there. But Kit hid his distress because Tod loved to aggravate, and Kit knew he would be sitting, now, waiting to be asked, 'Why on earth are you going...?'

Kit felt very tired. This relationship – the mauling, the one-upmanship, the concealment of feeling – was exhausting. It was a game of poker, and today he had no stomach for it. He wanted to cash in his chips; to lie in a feather bed; to swing in a hammock. The thought made him smile.

The front door was opened and shut, and Kit heard Alice in the hall, talking to Bones: 'I know it's cold, and I bet you're hungry... Hang on a tick while I take off my boots.'

Bones tiptoed into the room and stared at Tod, and a moment later Alice padded in wearing socks without shoes. Tod twisted round in his chair to her and, seeing him, she was brought up short in surprise.

For a moment Kit looked at her as if he were Tod, and had never met her before. She was dressed in such strange clothes, he thought with irritation: dark, shapeless layers which made her form indistinguishable, like a blackbird thar has puffed out his feathers on a cold day. Her face was white and her hair lank, dragged down around it. He felt disappointed, looking at her. He had expected some-one quite different to walk in.

'Oh!' she said. 'I didn't know anyone was here.'

'This is Alice,' said Kit, without moving. 'This is my father.'

Alice approached the wheelchair, transferring her house keys into her left hand and holding out her right. 'Hello.'

Tod took her hand and pulled her towards him to kiss her on the cheek. Kit could see Alice brace herself to resist and he felt a wave of anger. Was she going to make a fuss? And be embarrassing? Couldn't she at least pretend to be normal? In front of his father?

'I'm so glad to meet you,' said Tod, still clutching her hand. 'I hope we're going to get to know each other.'

'Yes,' she said, looking flustered, 'I hope so. How nice...' She glanced at Kit. 'I had no idea you were coming.'

'It was a surprise,' said Kit.

Tod looked from one to the other, enjoying himself. 'Now: what I intend to do,' he said to Alice, 'is have a quick word with Kit here – dull, family business – and then I thought we could go out to lunch?'

'I'm quite busy this morning, as it happens,' responded Kit.

'Yes, I assumed you would be,' said Tod, turning to him, 'so I'll take Alice, on her own. We can give Damita the rest of the day off – she's got a nephew in St John's Wood she wants to visit.'

Alice opened her mouth and shut it again. She looked at Kit for help, but he did not catch her eye. Instead, he reached for another cigarette, saying, 'Right,' and trying not to sound put out.

'We'll just get this dull business out of the way,' said

Tod, smiling one of his bared-tooth smiles at Alice.

Alice stared at him as if she were hard of hearing. 'Yes, of course,' she agreed in the end. 'I'll feed the dog and then I'll go and get dressed. Do you want me to book a table?'

Kit laughed, 'Don't worry, Dad's been going to the same restaurant for fifty years. They'll give him a table.'

He had not meant this to sound quite as aggressive as it did, and both Alice and Tod looked at him for a moment. Then, as if Kit had never spoken, Tod said to Alice, 'There's an Italian restaurant I adore, in Soho. We'll go there. Italian food is the best, isn't it?'

'Yes,' said Alice, looking nervous. 'Delicious.'

'If you love Italy so much,' asked Kit, chucking his cigarette into the fireplace, 'why do you live in Spain?'

'You always ask me that,' replied Tod with an edge to his voice, 'and the answer is that Ibiza is not really Spain, it is Ibiza. I've had a house on Ibiza for forty-five years,' he went on to Alice. 'It's my home. I'm not one of those retired people who's put a drawing pin on the map and bought a house there.'

'Alice's parents live in Florida,' said Kit.

'Do they?' asked Tod. 'Are you American?' He said it very slowly, emphasising each syllable, as if he were asking, 'Do you speak English?'

'No,' replied Alice. 'They retired there. They stuck a drawing pin on the map.' She tried to smile at Tod as she said it, but she could not.

Tod shot a look at Kit. 'Ghastly place, Florida,' he said without repentance. 'I suppose you miss them, do you?'

'Yes, no, well – it's the house, more than anything,' said Alice, making a tight fist around the key she still held in the palm of her hand. 'They moved a while ago, but they sold the house last year. It was still my home.'

'Was it?' questioned Kit, frowning at her, 'I thought you lived with Emmy?'

Alice waited a moment, and then said quietly, 'It felt like my home.'

'I've never understood people's attachment to houses,' said Kit. 'Particularly in cities. One London house is pretty much like another, after all.'

Alice looked down at her hands, saying nothing.

'I'm glad you think so,' Tod said, 'since that's exactly what I wanted to talk to you about. You see, I'm putting this house on the market – that's why I'm going to see your mother.'

If he had aimed to get Kit's attention, he succeeded. 'You're doing what?' said Kit, swivelling his head and staring at his father.

'Selling this house. It's ridiculous, to keep it. After all, I'm never here.'

'But I live here,' said Kit, astonished.

'Yes,' said Tod. 'You can buy it if you want. If you've got four million quid!' He laughed.

'What about the studio?'

'Don't get any ideas – I'm going to have it turned into a two-bedroomed cottage, and then I'll rent it out. Do you know, if I do that, the rent will pay Damita's salary? And a pension for her. Extraordinary.' He turned to Alice. 'When I bought that place it was a car repair shop, and now it's a gold mine, sitting there doing nothing.'

'It's not "sitting there doing nothing",' argued Kit. 'It's my studio.'

'It's my health insurance!' Tod burst out. 'Damita's future!' His voice rang with self-justification.

Alice's nervous glance fled from one to the other. 'I must feed this poor dog,' she said, 'and get dressed.' She went into the kitchen and Kit heard Damita's exclamation of greeting.

'All right then,' Kit turned to Tod, 'what the fuck is going on?'

'I don't think you're looking after that girl very well. She looks half-dead.'

'She's fine. Don't change the subject.'

'Oh, Christopher, don't be childish. It's business: a tax thing. This house is still my primary residence. Blah blah,' he waved a hand, 'boring.'

'No,' countered Kit in a cold voice, 'Not boring. *Fascinating.*'

'Well, *I'm* bored. I don't want to talk about it.'

'You really are...' Kit shook his head.

'You must be able to see that it doesn't make sense for me to keep a vast house in London that I don't use.'

'Stop saying that. *I* use it,' said Kit, looking at him.

'But you can't have thought you could live here for ever, like the next bloody duke or something. It's not Brideshead, for Christ's sake. After all, what did you just say? "One London house is pretty much like another"? And you've made plenty of money from flogging those pictures,' he continued, 'so why not buy yourself a home of your own? It would be the adult thing to do.'

'I can't see what reason you would have for doing this, beyond spite,' spat Kit, watching Tod lift his coffee cup between his fists and suck at his drink.

'You'll be amazed to hear this, Kit,' responded Tod,

'but not everything revolves around you, or is done deliberately to punish you. This is a business decision.'

'Right. So, what are you going to do with all that money?'

There was a pause before Tod said, 'You have a very cruel way about you, Kit, sometimes.' He replaced his coffee cup in its saucer. With a trembling hand, he drew a folded handkerchief from his pocket, shook it out and patted the corners of his mouth with it. Concentrating hard, he refolded the cloth into a neat square.

I will not fall for your routine, Kit thought, watching him.

At last Tod said, 'I want to give the money – some of it – to your mother. I never gave her anything when we got divorced and I don't want her to worry about money for the next thirty years, after I'm dead.'

'But she's fine,' protested Kit. 'That cooking school is a hit – finally. She's raking it in.'

At this Tod shook his head, saying, 'When did you become so hard? You were such a kind little boy.'

Kit was as shocked as if he had been slapped, but he managed to hide it, saying, 'I learned at the feet of the master', and turning his head to stub his cigarette in the ashtray.

In the basement Alice stared at her reflection in the bathroom mirror. How could she go out to lunch with that man? To a restaurant? She was finding it hard enough to string a sentence together. Surely Tod had noticed her zoning out, unable to answer even the simplest questions, staring at him like a stunned animal. And how could she

make him believe there was any sort of relationship between her and Kit? Did he not have eyes in his head?

She tried to pull herself together, applying make-up
and searching for suitable clothes on the clothes rail, but
everything was too big and she started to panic, doing up
one pair of trousers after another and watching all of them
slip down from her waist to hang on her hips, or off her
bottom. She scrabbled in a drawer for a belt and tucked
several jumpers into the waistband of the smallest pair of
trousers she could find. She would overheat, she knew,
in the restaurant, but she would have to bear it – or risk
detection.

She heard a tread on the stair and to her surprise, Kit's
voice. 'Can I come in?'

'One sec,' she said, making sure she was covered up.
'All right.'

He pushed open the door and stood in the doorway.
Alice did not know what to do. She folded her arms and
looked at him.

'You don't mind having lunch with Dad on your own,
do you?' Kit asked her. 'He'll be a lot nicer if I'm not
there.'

'No, well, yes. I mean, I do a bit. Do I have to?' Fear
curled inside her like a live snake.

'I'm not going to *make* you,' said Kit, exasperated,
'but – for God's sake, it's lunch in a restaurant. How bad
can it be? Anyway, what else have you got to do today?'

*Why did you ask me if I minded? You're not interested
in the answer*. Alice tried to gather her scattered wits and
respond, but all she could manage was, 'I just... don't
feel up to it.' It sounded pathetic. She was pathetic. If
she had not felt so weak, she could have put together an

argument. But then, she knew if she had not felt so weak, she would not have minded going to lunch.

'You don't feel like anything any more,' accused Kit.

'No, I don't,' she sighed, subsiding.

'You've got to stop behaving like such a victim,' went on Kit.

'Right.' She looked down at her discarded clothes. She was defeated.

When Kit looked at her expression it frightened him. He said, 'Now is not the time to have this conversation', and turned away from her, towards the stairs. Then he asked, 'Are you going to go, or not?'

'Yes, I'll go,' said Alice, in a more obedient voice. 'I'll be up in a minute.'

When Kit walked back into the sitting room Tod peered at him with narrowed eyes and then said, 'I remember that suit. It's rather a good one. Is that paint you've got on it?'

For a moment Kit didn't know what he was talking about, and then he looked down at what he was wearing. Of course, the trousers were his father's, left here long ago.

'You know,' continued Tod, annoyed, 'if you wear the trousers without the coat like that, you ruin the whole suit. They turn a completely different colour.'

'It's not a coat, it's a jacket.'

'Potatoes have jackets,' Tod countered with finality. Then he added, 'I hope the rest of my wardrobe is in better condition. Perhaps I'll take an overcoat away with me now – as usual it's bloody freezing in England.'

'Of course it is,' stopped Kit, with equal annoyance. 'It's March. Why don't you go to Gap and buy some new clothes? I'm sure they'd have an overcoat that would fit you.'

'What is "Gap?"', said Tod, suspicious.

'Don't be funny. Everyone knows what Gap is.'

'In any case. I can get a coat on Jermyn Street after lunch. Alice can help me.'

Alice made a cautious appearance in the doorway, saying, 'I'm ready', and standing on one leg to fiddle with the strap of her shoe.

Tod said, 'Good, we'll go.'

'Shall I drive?'

'No – it's easier for me to get in and out of a taxi. Run and hail one, would you?'

'You'll get one on Ladbroke Grove,' bossed Kit. 'Ask the driver to come round, and I'll get Dad down on to the pavement.'

'You talk about me as if I were a suitcase,' grumbled Tod.

And I a servant, thought Alice, her head spinning.

Outside, a few minutes later, Kit helped Tod ('Dammit, I can *manage*,') into the taxi, then he turned to Alice.

She looked so cold and frightened he had a sudden pang, of guilt, perhaps, or even sympathy. He pulled his scarf from his pocket to loop around her neck, 'Here, you look frozen.'

But Alice, far from feeling cherished, had the strangest feeling – that she was choking. 'Don't,' she cried in panic, taking a step back.

'What?' Kit snapped into anger. 'Fuck! I was giving you my scarf! Why do you have to be so *weird*?'

He turned on his heel and climbed the steps back up to the house. Alice watched him slam the front door, and then got into the taxi where Tod waited.

5

After lunch Tod told Alice there was an old friend he wanted to visit who lived around the corner in Meard Street, and Alice pushed him there in his wheelchair. She had to heave it on and off the kerbs and by the time they reached the front door she was feeling quite peculiar. She noticed her hand trembling as she reached to press the bell. It occurred to her that a banana and a mouthful of salad might not last the day if she was to be pushing Tod's wheelchair around London.

'What will you have?' Tod had said in the restaurant, snapping breadsticks and tossing the pieces into his mouth as if he were giving treats to a Labrador. 'Sometimes I have a veal chop with mashed potato, which is very good, and sometimes *gnocchi parmigiana*. You could have either of those. Something filling! You need fattening up.' He had eyed her up and down.

'D'you know,' Alice had replied, recoiling, 'I had such a late breakfast – I ate not long before I came back to the house. I'll probably have a salad.' She felt as if she were expected to pull up her sleeve and inject heroin, sitting here in front of him and in front of the whole restaurant. Sweat trickled down her ribcage.

'Salad! You can make that at home,' Tod had sniffed. 'At least have some mozzarella on it. They fly it in from Naples every morning. And wine, will you have wine? I'm going to have Campari and soda – does that tempt you?'

'Nothing to drink for me,' Alice had said. 'Just fizzy water.' Tod's mouth snapped shut on the *grissini* and she had known she was a disappointment to him.

From the intercom beside the front door on Meard Street came a squawk. 'It's me,' Tod shouted up at it. 'Let me in.' Alice heard a woman's laugh, and the door clicked.

It was a small block of flats, and in silence they took the lift to the top floor. Alice stared into the mirror and Tod looked down at his hands. It was very hot, and hotter still on the landing where they emerged. Alice unbuttoned her coat and, feeling tired out, steadied herself with a hand against the wall while Tod pushed himself across the carpet to a black-painted door. He nudged it open with his feet, calling, 'Rosie? I'm here.' Alice followed him into the flat and shut the door behind her.

It was quiet in this apartment, like being in a room high up in a Manhattan hotel, with the muffled sound of far-off traffic and the hum of something electrical, a computer or a fridge. The hall where they waited was theatrical: carpeted in thick green and the walls painted so dark a grey they might have been black. In the middle of the room stood a mirrored table on which rested an enormous crystal bowl containing lily-of-the-valley, whose scent reminded Alice of bath time at her grandparents' house. All at once she felt tears crowd her eyes. *No!* she thought in fury. *Pull yourself together.*

A door opened and a small, round woman stepped towards them, smiling, both hands held out in greeting. Alice guessed she was sixty-five or seventy, chic and urban, dressed in black and wearing a scarlet turban on her head. A large gold ring, the size of a walnut, stood proud on one finger. On her tiny feet were gold slippers.

'Tod Miller,' she said, 'am I happy to see you.' It was a statement of fact, rather than a question.

She kissed Tod on one cheek and stroked the lapels of his suit with the flat of her hands. Then she turned to Alice. 'I know who you are,' she said in a low, dramatic voice. 'You're Alice.'

'Hello,' said Alice, holding out her hand.

Rosie shook it and held on to it, 'But darling, aren't you a beauty? And a figure to *die* for, you lucky thing.'

Alice wanted to laugh out loud at the absurdity of this, but she managed to keep a straight face.

'Clever Kit,' Rosie went on to Tod, letting go of Alice's hand. 'Doesn't he always land on his feet?'

'Doesn't he just,' agreed Tod through pursed lips.

Rosie clasped her hands, saying, 'Come on then: tea and a haircut. Am I doing you both?' She led the way through a small sitting room, wallpapered in gold, and into the kitchen. Alice pushed Tod in her wake.

'I don't know,' replied Tod, 'I haven't asked Alice.'

Alice cleared her throat. 'Asked me what?'

'Rosie is a very famous hairdresser. As well as being a dear friend. When I come and see her she gives me a trim. If you're a very lucky girl, and you make a good impression, she might do you.'

'What an awful way of putting it,' said Rosie, with a throaty laugh. 'The poor girl will be completely put off!'

Alice searched for words, and found none. She felt as if she had been lifted off her feet and carried forth, like Alice by the Red Queen, into a world without order. To get her breath she looked around the kitchen.

After the bread-and-gruel of Tod's interior design and the chill of the March day outdoors, this apartment was like a fruit salad. The kitchen walls were painted a glossy orange, the floor was tiled in shiny, tobacco-coloured cork and rampant, green-leaved potted plants spilled out of their tubs. *But Tod must hate it here*, Alice thought, puzzled. It was the antithesis of his prized aesthetic.

A bamboo table stood in the window, piled high with newspapers and magazines, and the remains of a cheese and tomato sandwich lay abandoned on the *Guardian*. The crossword had been mostly filled in – she and Tod must have interrupted Rosie's lunch. Tod parked himself beside the table and peered down at the newspaper, tugging his spectacles out of his breast pocket. Alice took off her coat and hugged it in front of her, wondering where to put herself.

'Let's have champagne,' suggested Rosie, turning from the fridge with a bottle. 'Will you open it, Alice? And by the way, I won't be offended if you don't want me to cut your hair – take no notice of Tod.' She looked at Alice with her head on one side. 'But... have you ever had it short?'

'Not for years,' replied Alice, putting a hand up to her head in embarrassment.

'Hm,' mused Rosie, reaching three glasses down from a shelf.

'Hispaniola,' said Tod, tapping the crossword with his glasses. 'I would fill it in, but I can't hold the pen.'

'Hell and damnation. I can't believe you got that. It's been driving me crazy all morning. It's very impolite, you know,' she scolded, 'to finish someone else's crossword. It's like finishing the food on their plate.'

'Well, don't worry, I'm not going to eat the rest of that,' said Tod, gesturing at the sandwich.

'I expect you've had three courses at Il Posto,' said Rosie, pouting. 'You are mean not to have asked me along.'

'I didn't know until the last minute whether Kit would be joining us,' said Tod, 'but it turned out he was too busy. And anyway, it was nice to eat lunch with Alice. Get to know her.'

Alice, untwisting the wire on the champagne bottle, stared at him in amazement. Was that a joke? But no, he seemed to believe this was the case. She pulled the cork out of the bottle and Rosie held the glasses out to be filled.

'I always turn the bottle, not the cork,' said Tod to Alice, 'but you find it easier the other way, do you?'

'I don't expect it matters,' observed Rosie, glancing at Alice. 'What shall we drink to?'

'To us, of course,' replied Tod. They all raised their glasses.

'And next time you two have lunch,' Rosie said when she had had a sip, 'I expect to be invited. Will you promise, Alice? I know he won't keep his word.'

'Of course,' said Alice, turning from Tod to Rosie. 'It's a promise.'

She could not work out the dynamic between them – were they flirting? Their communications seemed to travel on a frequency she could not receive.

'Very good,' nodded Rosie, 'I'll hold you both to that. Now, I'll get my scissors and make a start on Tod's hair.'

She left the room. Quick as a flash, Alice tipped most of her champagne into the sink. She glanced at Tod, who had seemed to be absorbed by the newspaper, but now he was looking at her. Had he seen? She blushed.

But all he said was: 'If you look in the cupboard above the kettle you'll find a tin of nibbly things. Fetch it down, would you?'

Alice opened the cupboard door and sure enough, there was the tin. She passed it to Tod. 'I'm afraid you'll have to open it for me,' he said. 'My hands are useless.'

'Oh, I'm sorry, of course. How could she have forgotten? She had had to cut up his lunch for him. Slicing the veal chop off the bone had almost made her sick.

As Alice fished a handful of cheese straws out of the tin and passed them to Tod, she felt a wave of disgust that turned to fury. Food! Everything was about food, it was everywhere. Here they were, Tod about to have a haircut, and he was eating again, and it had been a matter of minutes since she had had to wrestle with the notion of lunch and how to get out of eating that. The sensation of buttery crumbs of pastry on her fingers made her skin crawl. She would never get away from food as long as she was around other people. She would have to move to a desert, or to the top of a mountain, or cut off her hands, or sew up her mouth –

'Here I am!' said Rosie, coming back into the room with her scissors, and spreading a newspaper on the floor.

She wheeled Tod's chair on to the centre of it and wrapped a towel around his shoulders, clipping it tight under his chin with a jag-toothed hairclip.

'Make sure you've covered everything,' grumbled Tod, 'because I hate having hair all over me and the chair afterwards.'

'Oh, *pff*,' breathed Rosie, fussing round him.

After spraying Tod's hair with an atomiser, Rosie put her head on one side and examined him. Then she took up her scissors and a comb and started to snip his hair in a brisk, rapid motion. Tod closed his eyes, soaking up the warmth of her attention as if he were sunbathing. They were all three silent for a few moments, luxuriating in the soft *clip-clip* sound of the scissors.

It occurred to Alice that Tod and Rosie seemed to have no catching up to do; they had no need for chat. They were as quiet and comfortable together as a couple who had been married – and happily – for decades.

'It's the one thing I miss,' Tod said.

'What, having your hair done?' asked Rosie.

'No, being touched. No one ever touches me – there's no need.'

'Poor old Fox,' soothed Rosie. 'What about kissing on

the cheek? Hello and goodbye?'

'I don't count that. What I mean is, the concentrated touch of another adult on my body.'

Rosie lifted an eyebrow. 'I hope you're not getting some kinky pensioner's thrill out of this.'

'Don't flatter yourself.'

Rosie tutted at him and tipped his head down so that she could cut the hair at the nape of his neck.

They are flirting, Alice thought, watching them.

'You should have a massage,' said Rosie. 'That's what I do, once a week. Someone comes to the house. It's heaven: for an hour and a half, someone concentrating on my saggy old body.'

Alice was warm and drowsy. The sound of the scissors, and of their gentle banter, was soporific. She looked out of the window to try and wake herself up.

The view was of a perfect *Mary Poppins* London: chimney pots; steep slate roofs; the black candelabra of plane trees silhouetted against the sky. Alice could see down into the building opposite where men and women sat in a large, shared office, the room lit by bright electric lights. A woman stood beside the printer, collecting each sheet of paper as it emerged, lost in thought. Alice was flooded by recognition: office life. She wondered if she would ever return to work. Just now, a future of any kind seemed quite out of her reach. It made her afraid, to think how far she had stepped away from the way other people spent their days. *I have become weird*, she thought, then she stopped herself.

You stupid girl, she chided, *this is what happens if you relax*. She closed her mind and turned to look at Tod. His eyes were still closed. Without his gimlet stare, wearing the towel like a cape and with pink neck and ears exposed, he looked elderly and vulnerable. The floor, and the towel around his shoulders, were dusted with snowy clippings.

'I'm going to leave it a bit longer than last time,' Rosie told him, 'because it's cold out, and I don't want you catching your death.' She unclipped the towel from around his shoulders and gently brushed his face and throat and the back of his neck. 'There you are, pet,' she said, holding out her hand, 'that'll be two hundred quid.'

Tod opened his eyes with reluctance. 'Let's call it lunch. Next time I see you.'

'I suppose that'll have to do,' Rosie sighed. 'I don't think I've ever got a penny out of him, you know,' she added to Alice.

'Ha!' he scoffed. 'You've cost me more than pennies.'

The remark, which Alice did not understand, hung in the air until Rosie said, 'Now, Alice, how do you feel?'

'Me?' said Alice, panicked. 'How do I feel?'

'Yes,' said Rosie, looking at her, 'about your hair? Would you like a trim? It wouldn't take long. You might as well.'

'Oh! No, no, really,' said Alice, laughing and waving her away, 'I'm fine. My hair is fine, don't worry about me, please.'

'I'm not worried,' said Rosie more sharply. '*I* don't care; it's your lookout.'

Alice blushed.

'Come on, Alice,' said Tod. 'Don't be difficult.'

Alice faltered. 'Well,' she said, 'What would you do? Nothing too radical…'

'Oh no,' replied Rosie, snick-snacking the air with her scissors. 'It only needs a bit of shape put back into it.'

6

Kit was asleep when Alice came back later that afternoon. He had not known what to do after they left and so he had drunk a glass of whisky and then gone to bed in his clothes, the duvet pulled up to his chin.

When he woke he did not, for a moment, remember what had happened earlier in the day. He knew there was a reason he felt anxious and dismayed. What was it? Then the memory flooded his brain: *my father; this house.* At once he was filled with the dark energy of rage and he could not remain lying down for another moment. He reared up in one furious motion and thundered downstairs to the kitchen. There was no sign of Alice. His hand hovered between the kettle and the whisky bottle. He switched on the kettle and then, letting out a little groan, he leaned his palms on the table, his head and chest weighted with anger.

A few moments after the taxi containing Alice and his father had driven them away to lunch, Kit had exhaled and let his shoulders uncramp from around his earlobes. He had stared at the space where his father's wheelchair had stood as if a stain had been left on the floor.

The house felt full of spies. The building was no longer his friend and nor would Alice be when she came back from lunch. This was what happened: Kit was stripped of anything precious, as a matter of course.

How foolish he had been to begin to imagine, having lived there alone for so many years, that the house might have become his by default.

Tod was greedy and sentimental but abhorred and punished such weaknesses in others. This capricious behaviour was therefore characteristic and Kit had suffered before at the whim of such decisions. 'That bed,' his father had said down the telephone a year or so ago, 'in my bedroom. I've sold it to a nice man in California who saw it in *Interiors*.'

'When you say "nice", you mean "rich", right? And, when you say "that bed", do you mean you've sold the design? Or the actual bed?'

'The *bed*, the *bed*,' Tod had repeated with impatience.

'The one I sleep in?'

'It's not *yours*, though, is it?' Tod had said. 'I designed it, I certainly paid for it – Christ, I practically built it. Look, he's going to ring you up about it. You'll have to arrange for it to be shipped. Buy yourself another one, why don't you? They relaunched them the other day. They're not expensive.'

He knows the price of everything and the value of

nothing, Kit had thought with bitter resignation. He wanted to throw the telephone across the room but instead he said, 'Yes, Dad.'

In the kitchen Kit saw that Damita had chucked out the fishes' dirty water, polished the bowl and put them back. They looked refreshed, nosing at the clean glass. Kit had frowned at them, annoyed. *Not my bed, not my house, not my fish.*

He had opened the connecting door and crept downstairs into Alice's bedroom. All this stuff, everywhere! Like debris left by a tide. Her discarded clothes, strewn on chairs. Pots of moisturiser, their lids left off, scattered on the bathroom shelf. A wet towel hooked over the shower rail. Her toothbrush, resting on its side in a puddle of opaque water.

He had stood in the doorway and looked but he had not touched anything, as if he had been standing at the scene of a crime. Bones, sleeping, lay like a corpse across the bed.

Now Kit turned from leaning and groaning at the table to see, through the kitchen window, Alice looking at him from the garden. Their eyes met and they regarded each other for a moment as if they were strangers, standing on opposite platforms at a railway station. When the dog had at last squatted for a pee, Alice came back into the house and then into the kitchen.

'What happened to your hair?' asked Kit.

Alice put a hand up to her head. She looked puzzled,

as if she herself was unsure how it had happened. 'We had lunch, me and your dad. And we went to visit a friend of his. She cut my hair.'

'Rosie. He took you to see Rosie.'

'Yes. I didn't really want... But they... she... I couldn't say no, somehow.'

There was a pause, then Kit said, 'She was my father's mistress.'

'What?'

'Yes. Mistress, girlfriend, whatever.'

He made himself a cup of tea and Alice stood, waiting for more. As he stirred in the milk Kit said, 'Poor old Mum – she didn't stand a chance against Rosie. No one would – that woman's got a hide like leather.' His description made Alice wince.

'Did she leave? Your mum?'

'Yes. He wouldn't give her any money to go with, of course, and she didn't have any of her own, so it took ages. He wanted her to stay put, and keep quiet. He kept telling me she was going to be destitute.'

'What happened to you?'

'I stayed here. Mum asked me if I wanted to go with her, and I said no. I moved into the basement; it got pretty rank in the house. Dad spent most of his time at Rosie's.'

Alice registered an enormous, ungovernable distance between herself and Kit, a gap that seemed to widen with every word he spoke.

'I didn't know,' she said.

'You couldn't have known,' said Kit, shrugging. 'But that's what my father does. He likes to separate people.'

Then Alice, taking a deep breath, said, 'He's asked me

to drive him to Cornwall. To your mum's.'

Kit laughed, shaking his head. 'You see? Of course he has!'

'What shall I do?'

'Take him, if you like,' Kit shrugged. 'You've nothing else to do, have you? There's nothing to keep you here.'

Alice looked at him, and then out of the window. She said she supposed he was right.

Part Three

1

So Tod and Alice, and Bones lying across the back seat of the car, went to Cornwall.

Neither Kit nor Tod could – or wanted to – give Alice directions, so she got them off the internet, typing in the name of Iona's house, Trebartha, which meant 'north hill', and then peering at the satellite picture on the screen.

The house stood a few miles inland of the north coast. In the image Alice could even see the walled kitchen garden and its neat rows of vegetables.

Alice knew next to nothing about Iona, gathering from Kit (who described his mother, on the rare occasions he spoke of her, as 'that hopeless woman') that she had been a model when she had met his father, that she was much younger than Tod, that she had been pregnant with Kit when she had married, and that now she ran a business teaching people how to grow and cook their own garden produce.

In the car Tod said, 'She's a vegetarian,' wrinkling his nose and staring out of the window.

He was a demanding companion – Alice was tired out before they hit the motorway. He wanted the car hotter, then colder; he wanted fresh air, but not to sit in a draught; he wanted to stop for tea and biscuits, but not for petrol ('I can't think why you didn't fill the tank before we set off').

Of course, he was accustomed to being looked after: Damita did everything for him, and seemed to have no demands of her own. She had a husband on Ibiza, but they had never had children. 'Why not?' asked Alice.

'I've no idea,' said Tod, surprised by the question. 'Perhaps they didn't want them.' But Damita had worked for him for nearly twenty years and Alice wondered whether, in fact, Tod was the reason there were no children. She could not imagine how Damita could have time in her life for anything other than Tod.

Alice was feeling peculiar and finding it hard to concentrate on what Tod was saying. She had undertaken her usual regime this morning – banana, walk with Bones – but then she had had to pack an overnight bag, to drive into the West End and pick Tod up from the hotel, to transfer him, his luggage and the wheelchair into her car – thankfully, with the help of the doorman – and now to concentrate on driving. There had been no sign of Kit.

After these extra activities and the corresponding upset to the fine balance of her mental equilibrium, she was tired out. She had a nasty feeling she might have to eat something soon, or risk a faint: there had been a buzzing in her ears when she had settled Tod in his seat and done up the seatbelt around him. Now she was worried that if they stopped at a service station she would find nothing she could eat in the shop. *If the worst comes to the worst,* she told herself, *I could have an apple.*

In the event she and Tod made it to Trebartha with no further stops. At the end of a narrow lane, beside a square grey manor house that loomed in the dusk, Alice emerged from the car, stiff from the long drive, and stretched. She looked up at the house and breathed in the cold air. It felt like a draught of iced water. Tod opened the passenger door and began to struggle to his feet as Iona stepped towards them out of the glow of the porch light.

Alice was ambushed by Iona's looks. She was glamorous – it had nothing to do with age or having been a model. She simply *was,* and to a degree that had always embarrassed her: she was one of those women that other people stared at, in shops. It was the way she was made.

She must be sixty, Alice guessed, or very near it. Her steel-grey hair was short and blown about and her skin looked extraordinarily soft, as if she anointed it every evening. ('I do,' she told Alice later, 'with rosehip oil.')

Iona had battled for years to get anyone interested in her vegetable business but now the courses were booked out every week. It seemed everyone wanted to get mud under their fingernails. Even in winter people came and learned that their own garden, treated with respect, could keep them well fed in January. 'It's all about nurture,' Iona said that evening, when she was showing Alice around. 'Everything is. I know it sounds feeble and unsophisticated, but it's true.' She smiled at Alice.

On the gravel she said, 'Tod! And you, you're Alice.' She kissed Alice – a firm, old-fashioned kiss – and clasped her to her chest. 'You poor thing, you've had an awful time.'

There it was! Out there, and she'd just arrived. Alice felt as if she had been turned upside down, rinsed, and righted again. Iona was abrupt but somehow soothing.

'Come on,' continued Iona. 'Let's get inside, it's freezing. She looked towards the sky in anxiety, and then towards the garden. 'I hope my poor boys have got off home.' Getting his wheelchair out of the boot she said, 'Here we are, Tod.'

'Don't put it on the gravel,' he barked at her. 'You won't be able to push it. Put it on the flagstones and then help me get there. We should have parked closer to the house.'

'Shall I move the car?' asked Alice.

'No, it's too late, I'm out now.'

'Come on, Tod, it's only a yard or so,' coaxed Iona, stepping round him like a wary cat. Alice gave Tod her arm and he used her as a prop for the few strides it took him to get across the gravel to his chair. As soon as he was sitting in it, Iona took the handles and pushed him into the house.

Alice remained outside, alone for a moment. She stared up at the darkening sky as Bones climbed from the car. The dog stretched before tiptoeing over to a row of lavender bushes beside the house and sniffing them one by one. Rooks coughed in the trees above; Alice breathed in the damp, cool air, and with it in her lungs she felt, *I am here*.

She joined the others in the kitchen and Iona asked her, 'Will you have tea? Or a drink?'

'Tea, please,' said Alice.

Iona switched on the kettle and then removed a brown dish from the Aga. She took off its lid, shaped like a witch's hat, and gave the contents a stir.

'What about me?' asked Tod.

'I assumed you'd have a drink,' said Iona, turning away from the pot with her wooden spoon. 'Is it Campari, still?'

'Yes,' replied Tod.

'Well, you'll have to wait a moment – I want to show Alice the garden, before it gets dark.'

'And what am I supposed to do?' asked Tod, making a petulant moue of his mouth.

'We won't be a minute,' said Iona, pacifying him. Or was she antagonising him? Alice could not be sure, and in any case she was distracted by the cooking pot, whose contents Iona was attending to. *What was in there?* Alice had forgotten for a moment that she would have to negotiate the minefield of someone else's cooking. And she was so hungry! The smell in the kitchen was making her dizzy. Perhaps she could eat it. *Yes*, she told herself. *I'll eat it.* It seemed so obvious: she was hungry; there was food; she could eat.

Iona put the dish back into the Aga and filled the teapot. Then she turned to Alice. 'Come with me,' she said, picking up a torch and a coat.

Alice followed her outside, shivering. They crossed the lawn to a stone wall, where an iron handgate creaked as

Iona opened it and led the way into the field. 'There are usually cows, so you have to keep the gate shut. But they're still indoors at the moment – they'll come out again when it warms up.'

'Right,' said Alice, trying to sound enthusiastic. She was so cold! She wanted to go to bed and never get up again.

A few yards into the field they stopped and stood. 'Look,' said Iona, switching off the torch, 'there's the sea.'

Alice, looking down, could just make out the blurred, dark shapes of the hills and woods that lay below them and then, at the horizon, a flat, luminous disc.

'Funny it's always silver like that,' mused Iona, 'as if it had its own private light source.'

'Isn't it the moon?'

'No, there's no moon tonight,' responded Iona in her brisk way. 'Come on: supper time.'

Alice had promised herself she would eat whatever was in the pot but when the time came and the loaded plate stood in front of her, she could not. Instead, she tore a piece of bread into pieces, sipped at a glass of wine and picked up her fork and put it down again. She suspected this charade was futile: Iona was no fool.

As challenging as not to eat was not to allow the bitter conflict that raged in her head to show on her face. As soon as she could she jumped up and cleared their three plates, rushing to scrape everything into the bin. Thank God, now she could relax – unless there was pudding, in which case the pantomime would begin again.

Iona smoked a long, slender reefer with slow relish. 'One of my garden boys makes them for me. It stops everything hurting. Gardening is torture, you know, for old ladies like me, and yet we're the ones who love it most! It's very unfair.'

Tod was disapproving, and refused to have a puff when Iona offered it.

'It would help you, with the pain.'

'So I'm told,' replied Tod in a crushing tone. 'People like you are always trying to force marijuana on me.'

'How annoying for you,' said Iona, regarding him and puffing out smoke.

'What do you think of Alice's hair?' asked Tod.

'I love it. But then, I love short hair. One of the best things about being old is having short hair and no one minding.'

'Rosie cut it,' said Tod in triumph, 'Yesterday. We went and had tea with her. She and Alice are great friends.'

Alice was mortified. 'Hardly –' she began, and then stopped and looked down, turning her glass of mint tea in her palm.

'Those glasses came from Marrakesh,' Iona told her, 'like the tagine.'

'Do you remember our trip to Marrakesh?' asked Tod. 'Marvellous, wasn't it? It all seemed so exotic, then. When was that?'

'Oh, so long ago,' replied Iona, but left it there. Alice could tell from her voice that she had no wish to reminisce.

'We stayed with Peter Katz, didn't we?'

Iona said nothing.

'Well,' demanded Tod, 'didn't we?'

'Yes, we did,' said Iona. 'In that beautiful house he had, full of birds.'

'That's right. It's coming back to me now: we had a row about some stupid little thing.' He looked at Iona, but she was staring into the fire. Tod turned to Alice with a bland smile. 'Probably something about his wife.'

After a moment Iona turned to Alice and said, 'Poor child, you look exhausted. Let me show you where you're sleeping.'

They climbed up two flights of stairs and Iona showed Alice into a large, bare room with a bed, an armchair and a row of hooks on the wall for her clothes. There was a bathroom on the landing. 'Get up when you like and help yourself to whatever you want for breakfast – there are no rules here. You must take what you want, when you want it.'

'Thanks,' said Alice. So her habits had not gone un noticed. She wanted to acknowledge the sensitivity, to bond with Iona, but she seemed to have forgotten how to communicate. She felt worn out. She fiddled with the strap of her overnight bag, and managed to say, 'I'm sorry about Rosie, and the haircut. I didn't know, until Kit told me afterwards, about…' she tailed off. Then she added, 'Tod's not very… kind, is he?'

'No, kind he is not.' Then she said, 'I think it maddens him that he can't upset me any more.'

'Is he always so mean? Kit said he was, but I couldn't believe it.'

'Oh, is he still like this with Kit? How sad. Yes, I'm afraid so. Sometimes it may look like he's not, and it may sound like he's not… but somewhere, in everything he says, there's a hidden piece of glass. I'd love to say, "It's because of the wheelchair", but he was always like that. The only thing that changes is whether it hurts.' Then she looked at Alice. 'But Kit's not cruel, is he?'

'No,' Alice frowned. 'Not cruel.'

'I wish Kit weren't so angry with me.' There was a pause. Perhaps she wanted to open a discussion, but Alice was stupid with tiredness and could not think what to say. 'Well, goodnight,' said Iona then, squeezing Alice's elbow and going back down the stairs.

In bed, wearing her woolly hat to keep the cold off her shorn head, Alice wondered for a moment, *Perhaps I could stay here?* A part of her longed to. She imagined swimming in the sea, walking, gardening, eating toast in the kitchen (eating! Always eating, in her fantasy life!), helping Iona somehow... being useful. But then she remembered her regime, and she knew it would be impossible. Other people's houses were full of irregularities – and Iona taught cookery, for heaven's sake. There would be food everywhere, it would be ungovernable. She could not stay. There would be communal meals, other people looking at her, shared life, cakes and biscuits... No, it was impossible. She had to get back to her basement.

Bones, in the armchair, waited until Alice had switched the light off and then climbed on to the bed, collapsing next to Alice and giving a long sigh, which made Alice smile. *Bones would like to stay*, she thought.

She turned on to her side. If she slept on her back it was sore in the morning, as if she had been sandpapered. *Today was a successful day*, she thought with satisfaction. *Nothing disorderly, or out of turn.* She hoped she could remain as vigilant tomorrow.

Sometimes she imagined what Emmy would say if she

could hear these thoughts. She would be puzzled, asking, *But what's the aim? What's the point?*

Alice wondered what the answer to that was. *It's like doing the same exam every day*, she thought to herself. *Sometimes I pass, and sometimes I fail.* It didn't matter which, because the next day she set herself the same exam.

2

In the morning Alice woke shivering. It was still dark. She reached out to turn on the light and look at the clock: not quite six. Steeling herself, she took a deep breath, got out of bed, switched on the electric heater and ran to the bathroom for a pee.

'Fuck! Cold!' she said aloud, seeing her breath hang in puffs in the air.

She grabbed her bag of clothes and put everything on: several sweaters, tights, leggings and jeans. Then she rummaged in the bedclothes for her hat, which had come off in the night, and put that on too.

'Come on Bones,' she called, and the dog shifted herself into a standing position on the mattress and then flumped on to the floor to perform a complicated routine of stretches concluding with a yawn, a sneeze and a shake of the head.

Alice tiptoed downstairs in her socks and Bones skee-tered behind her on the wooden stairs. 'Shush,' said Alice to her. From the sitting room, as they passed the door, came a loud snore. Tod must be sleeping there.

In the kitchen the warmth was tranquillising but she did not allow herself to enjoy it. She had a job of work to do: first the banana, and then the walk. She had to get out before someone stopped her.

She looked around for a fruit bowl. Surely this veg- etarian must have a banana somewhere in the house? But then again, she thought with a sinking heart, it was all about local and sustainable here, and bananas were nei- ther. She gave up her search and drank a glass of water instead, thinking to herself, *This is why I have to go back to London.*

Finding a coat and a pair of boots by the back door, she put them on and stepped outside. She took the path she and Iona had taken the night before, across the garden and into the field.

There was a sagging old caravan parked in the corner of the field beside the gate and Alice peered in through its windows as she passed it, taking in the mouldy interior and the fly-speckled window sills. *I could live here,* she thought. She turned from it to the view and stood mes- merised, staring at the landscape which emerged from the dawn and feeling the wind buffet her from top to bottom and somehow pass through her, as if she were a house with open windows. It was still half dark and the ground that fell away from her was blurred and indeterminate, like a pool of water she might dive into. She could not see the sea this morning.

She took deep breaths and felt herself expand with energy – the air itself was sustenance. She set off down the hill through the wet grass to a wall made of slate slabs, stacked in tilted rows, that stood between the field and the wood. As she approached the wall she saw a place where stones had been left poking out to make a ladder. She pulled herself up and over, jumping down into the dead leaves that lay banked against the wall on its other side.

Now she was in the woods.

Bones, landing on the ground beside her, froze for a moment and then bolted, flashing in and out of sight between the trees and disappearing down the hill before them. Alice opened her mouth to call her back, and then shut it again. What did it matter? This was what dogs did.

She followed Bones's lead, downhill and along a narrow path, at least a path of sorts, marked by paw- and hoofprints. Alice could hear the tops of the trees clacking together and groaning in the wind, but down here it was quiet. Nothing seemed to move when she looked straight at it but she had the sensation of teeming life all around her and indeed she caught, from the corner of a glance, a deer rocking away, picking a neat path through the trees and over the broken ground, its coat the colour of singed paper.

Alice had to steady herself on tree trunks as the path was steep, falling in zigzags between the trees. She could hear and see the river at the bottom – brown water, grey stone, green ferns with their tips dipped into the water – and then she skidded the last few feet and stood beside it. Looking at the water, she felt breathless, as if it were carrying her away with it to the sea. She was surprised, when she turned her head away, that the wood behind her stood silent and still.

The path seemed to run alongside the river on the valley bottom, sometimes hopping over it to continue on the other bank. At first the stream was little more than a few feet across, but it became bigger, noisier and more self-satisfied as other streams joined it from the hillside. Alice stopped every now and again to look up at the treetops, or down into the water. She felt dizzy, at one point shaking her head and murmuring, 'What is going on?'

Just then the dog appeared in front of her, panting and shaking herself. Alice looked at her. 'Steady, Bones, you'll give yourself a heart attack,' she said. The yellow dog gave her a sideways look before turning and bolting off again.

Alice shoved her hands into the pockets of her coat and plodded on beside the river. She supposed she would come to the sea in the end. It hadn't looked far, last night, from the top of the hill.

When she reached the end of the woods there was another wall and another stile to climb over. She emerged into a flat grass field through which the river cut a broad path. Alice crossed the field and let herself out through a gate, then up a short, stony lane and into a churchyard. She whispered to Bones to walk beside her heel.

The church stood above her: ivy reaching up its walls; a dark yew standing on either side of the porch; tilted gravestones. Alice looked down from the churchyard and saw that her river led to a village – well, a handful of white houses – clustered around a bridge under which the river rushed towards the sea. There was no one about – *it might still be before eight*, she thought. She tiptoed down the lane from the church and through the village without seeing a soul.

At the bridge a well-worn path led away uphill between stunted bushes. A wooden sign read 'Cliff Path' and Alice followed it. As she climbed she was buffeted by gusts of wind, and when the path turned a corner she reached the edge of the cliff and felt its full force. All the air was blown out of her but then she began to take in great gulps. *I could live on this stuff*, she thought.

She sat on a bench a few yards back from the cliff's edge. Tears sprang to her eyes. *It's the wind*, she thought, searching Iona's coat pockets for a tissue and finding a wad of kitchen roll and half a Kit Kat. She mopped her eyes and nose.

Beneath her there was no beach, no strip of yellow sand at all. In front of her feet lay the springing grasses and then a sheer, vacant drop to the seething water. But to Alice the black cliffs and the slate-coloured sea, which she saw spread below, seemed not hostile but essential. Down there the water rose and fell, gasping, clutching and breathing in private, endless debate with the rocks.

Those secret, self-contained and wordless places, inaccessible, were the places Alice wished she could inhabit. Not up here, where the bench stood, where the air was breathed by other people – 'Ellen who loved this place', said a brass plaque on the bench – but the dark, hollow rocks where the cliff met the sea.

It was not enough, she realised now, to walk in the woods, or on the Scrubs, or to look at the sea. To *be* the woods, to *be* the rock, to *be* the water – that was the state she wished she were in. No more feeling, thinking or speaking. Not to matter; to *be* matter.

She sat until Bones came sidling up and looked at her, shivering, *Take me home*, and then sat heavily on one of Alice's feet, to draw her attention. Alice patted the dog's head, thinking, *I must feed poor Bones*, and got up. Her head swam; she had been in a trance. What had she been thinking of?

She was cold, now, and all at once, frightened. She did not feel strong – perhaps it was the battering of the wind, the earth and the sea that was making her feel feeble, but the thought of the walk back up the hill to Trebartha alarmed her. She was angry as she steadied herself against the wind with a hand on the back of the bench. *It's fine*, she told herself. *It's not too far. And when I get back I'll have some breakfast.* Something like porridge, she imagined, setting off down the path, with Bones treading in her footsteps.

After this walk, and no breakfast – and indeed no lunch or dinner yesterday – surely, she reasoned, she could let herself have *something* to eat, some little thing? As she trod downhill she could feel her heart fluttering, and her knees trembling with each step. When she held out a hand to open the gate she could see her fingers quivering. *Yes,* she reflected, *I'll need to eat something when I get back.*

All at once her brain felt sluggish and her thoughts floundered in her head like netted fish. She was confused. She prayed she would not encounter anyone on the path – she knew she would find it hard to speak, to respond, even to exchange a 'Good morning'. She could think of the words, her mouth would open, but gibberish might come out. She would need to lie down and rest before she saw Tod or Iona.

Once out of the wind, in the lee of the cliff, she felt stronger. As she continued to tread a steady path back through the village and the churchyard – back towards the river – she encouraged herself. Feeling ill like this, she reasoned, meant her body was having to *work*, just as it ought. This was achievement.

But on the lane below the churchyard it began to rain, and by the time she reached the woods she was soaked. She dragged herself over the stile, jumped down and staggered, losing her balance. How odd. Her legs were shaking. For a moment her head was filled with sound like a shaken-up bottle of fizzy water.

She began to labour back up the path. She had not noticed its gentle slope as she had descended, but now that she was walking in the other direction, tired and hungry, it felt steep. A cold sweat had broken out under her hair on the crown of her head. She thought of all her hair, cut off and left on Rosie's kitchen floor, and she wanted to cry.

This had been a stupid idea, she realised. She had come too far; she was weak; she was pathetic; she was like an elderly person or an invalid. Cursing herself, she continued to walk up the valley, placing one foot in front of the other and not looking up.

After a few hundred yards she had to stop again and lean against a tree trunk. She looked down at her trembling legs. *What's wrong with you?* she thought in anger. The yellow dog looked up at her, puzzled. 'What?' Alice asked it. 'Go away. Hunt rabbits or something: stop following me.' Her tongue felt thick and lazy in her mouth.

She tried to continue walking but a little further on she began to hear a buzzing in her ears and she realised she had almost ground to a halt, the steps she was taking were so small. Her legs were as heavy as if they were filled with sand, and she started to feel sick. She crouched on the ground and hung her head. Her heart fluttered in her chest like a bird caught in the rafters, as if it might spring through the bars of her ribs and fly away. This was such a clear image, such a live sensation, it was almost hallucinatory, and Alice began to panic.

'Oh, Bones,' she said out loud, 'I feel bad.'

She knelt on the ground and tucked her feet under her, as if in devout prayer. She was wet, now, all over: soaked from above by the rain and below by the wet ground. She breathed in the drenched smell of leaves and earth, staying motionless in her prayer-pose, wondering what would happen next. When she looked up at the path, a few minutes later, it was like a tendril, disappearing into the wood. How would she ever follow it? She wished there were crumbs scattered on the ground, like in Hansel and Gretel, and she could eat them.

Then she remembered the remains of the Kit Kat in Iona's coat pocket. Perhaps she could eat that? She pulled it out and unfurled the paper wrapper, and then the foil. There was half left.

Half a Kit Kat would get her back to the house – a quarter would do it. She would eat it. But first, she squinted at the paper. There was the nutritional information: she could read that and see exactly what was in it.

A hundred grams of Kit Kat would give her 26.1 grams of fat. More than a quarter of a Kit Kat was fat? How disgusting. She peered again at the label.

Her brain was moving like sliding mud; she could barely do the maths. *Come on*, she told it, *keep up*. She was holding in her hand half of a Kit Kat. According to the label that meant a weight of about ten grams. A quarter of that would be fat: just over three grams.

That was a lot. She looked at it again – maybe there was a bit less than a half left? Perhaps she could walk quickly, once she had eaten it, then she might work it off as she climbed the hill back to the house. She hovered in her crouching position, longing to eat but unable to put it in her mouth. She could imagine the chocolate softening on her tongue but she knew that when she had eaten it she would be just as hungry as before. And she would be disgusted with herself.

This was ridiculous, she thought. She *had* to eat it. How would she get home if she didn't? She took it out of the wrapper, put the foil back in her pocket and stood up, holding it between her fingers.

She looked at it. Then she threw it into the river.

There! Now there was no decision to be made; she would have to make it home. She was just a bit tired, that was all it was. She would be home in an hour, and she would feed poor Bones, and drink some tea, and all would be well. She and Bones could go back to bed and have a rest. Perhaps no one would know she had ever been out.

She bent over and put her head between her knees, taking deep breaths, then with a supreme effort, she trod onward up the path, placing one foot in front of the other, staring at the ground below her feet. In this way, as if she were at the end of a mighty pilgrimage, she made her way back through the wood.

At the bottom of the hill, below the field, she paused and looked up. It seemed to be an almost sheer climb to the wall where the stile was. She could see her footprints, where she had skidded downhill earlier. Had it been today? Had it been her? She could not have said for certain.

She began to pull herself up the hill, from tree to tree, using her arms. Blood thudded in her ears. Her head was splitting with pain and her legs were shaking, as useless as strands of spaghetti. She set her jaw and told herself, *Get moving!* She imagined soldiers in battle, not wanting to move, thinking they didn't have the strength – but they always did, didn't they? She was being pathetic, she would *make* herself do this.

The wall appeared in front of her as she had always known it would. *You see!* She said to herself. *You do have the strength – you have to force yourself, and not be so lazy. You didn't need that Kit Kat.* She pulled herself up, steadied herself at the top and looked up the field. She had made it.

She sprang off the top of the wall and landed in the grass but then, all at once, her legs buckled and she fell forward on to the ground. *Oh! What's happening?* She told herself to get up but her body would not obey her. It seemed to have collapsed, like a cardboard box in the rain, and lost its usefulness. It was all she could do to lift herself to her knees. She knelt in the grass and Bones came and snuffled her head. 'Bones!' mumbled Alice. Her voice was thick and unlike itself. She wanted to cry but she could not; she was too tired; it would take too much effort.

She put her arms around the dog's neck for a moment, leaning her face into Bones's coarse, yellow coat, but

Bones leapt away, thinking it was a game. Alice groaned and toppled forward, feeling sick, into the grass. A rushing sound like an untuned radio filled her head. Through this tumultuous noise she could hear her brain continue to command her: *Get up! Move! Walk! What are you doing? You can't lie here! Don't be so hopeless!* But her poor hungry body took no notice, and she slipped away unconscious, to a place where that shouting voice could not be heard.

3

Iona telephoned Kit to tell him. He did not recognise her voice, perhaps because it was strained with worry. 'If you come now,' she said, 'you could stay the night and take Tod to the airport in the morning. You must be desperate to see her.'

Kit probed himself for feelings, desperate or otherwise. He hoped he was, at least, coughing up the right responses. 'I'll come right away,' he said.

But he dawdled, smoking, in a state of anxiety, until the middle of the afternoon. Even when he got on the road he drove at a sedate pace, holding the steering wheel with both hands and leaning over it like an old woman. He, Iona and Tod had not been in the same room for more than two decades. *Bloody Alice*, he thought with savagery.

He wondered what it was, exactly, that had happened. Iona had said 'exhausted'. Kit was dubious. Tired girls did not go to hospital; they went to bed.

It's not my fault, he told himself, sitting in the café of the motorway services.

'It's no one's fault,' Iona said when he arrived.

She blames me, thought Kit.

'It's too late to visit the hospital now,' said Iona. 'You could see her in the morning, before you go. Or you could come back? I don't know. Tod's flight is at six.' She was tired, slopping wine into glasses for them both. Kit stood leaning on the Aga, and Bones lay supplicating at his feet. She had been pleased to see him but, 'I haven't forgiven you,' Kit had told her, and she had slunk away.

Iona sat at the kitchen table and turned the rings on her fingers. 'Tod's asleep. Thank God. He was in a foul temper. Furious I couldn't persuade Damita –' She bit her lip.

'Persuade Damita to do what?'

'Well,' she hesitated, 'originally he wanted, I mean he asked me to get Damita to drive here and pick him up. But her nephew wouldn't let her take the car – said he didn't want her driving on an English motorway in a strange car, so –'

'So Dad had to make do with me.' Kit stirred himself, patting his pockets for cigarettes.

'I had to reach you anyway,' pleaded Iona, 'because of Alice.'

Then she told him what had happened: that one of her boys, Jory, his name was, had arrived for work and switched off his car radio to hear a dog barking over and over in the field. Jory had opened up the offices, made coffee and gone out to feed the chickens. He had realised that the dog was still barking so he went into the field to look and found what he had at first thought was nothing more than a coat left out in the rain.

'Oh, dear God,' Iona had said when Jory had carried Alice into the kitchen. She had wiped the rain off Alice's white, still face, while he rang for an ambulance.

'I can't believe it was this morning,' Iona frowned, spreading her hands on the table and looking down at them. 'It feels like another lifetime.'

'What did the doctor say?' asked Kit.

'That she should stay in hospital for a few days, and in bed for at least a week.'

'And then what?'

'And then... I don't know,' Iona said, keeping her voice neutral.

'So, what's actually wrong with her?'

Iona looked up. 'I told you: I think she's exhausted.'

That word again. 'But,' Kit frowned. *Exhausted from what?* He kept that to himself, saying instead, 'Are you happy for her to stay here? For a week?'

'Of course, and you'll come back, won't you? Once you've put Tod on the plane?'

'Probably, yes. If that's what she wants.'

Iona said nothing more.

Kit took a Campari and soda into the sitting room where his father was resting. 'Dad?' he said in the dark, standing in the doorway. 'It's me, Kit. I've got a drink for you.'

'Put the light on, will you?' came Tod's voice. 'I can't find the blasted switch.'

Kit groped forward, finding a table with a lamp on it. He turned it on and stared at his father in dismay.

Iona had moved a bed in there and Tod lay on his back on top of the blankets like a bit of twisted metal. His limbs were skewed and his clothes rucked up around his armpits and knees. His face was creased with pain. The empty wheelchair waited at the end of the bed like a ghastly full stop. He stirred himself, attempting to reach a more upright position by pulling the cushions and pillows behind him into a tottering bolster, but then several of them tumbled to the floor and he started huffing and puffing with temper. Kit dithered, holding the glass.

'Don't just stand there, help me, for God's sake,' roared Tod, but when Kit stepped forward he could do nothing right: 'Not there, *there*, dammit,' and then, 'All right; *all right, I said*. Leave the glass on the table. Did you bring a straw?'

'She doesn't have any.'

'Wretched woman.' He sucked at his drink. 'You know I came all the way here to tell her about the money, and she doesn't want it? Says she won't take it. Completely wasted journey.'

'So –'

'No,' snapped Tod, 'that doesn't mean I'm going to keep the house. I'll give the money to Rosie. She'll appreciate it.'

Kit swelled almost to bursting point with rage. All of a sudden he had a splitting headache.

'Mum says dinner is in ten minutes,' he said, when he

could trust himself to speak. 'Do you need me to help you into your chair?'

'Help? Ha! *That's* what you call it.'

'All right, I'll see you in the kitchen.'

Of the three of them Tod was the most fortunate, reflected Kit as he sat beside the fire in the kitchen and watched Iona lay the table, because he did not doubt himself. How did he manage that? Kit was envious. He could see from his mother's expression that she was dreading dinner – the event – just as he was, but Tod? No, Tod was sitting up in bed, finishing off his Campari, and thinking about dinner in terms of food and drink.

It made Kit laugh when he read columns in the newspapers about how the nation could restore its core values by going back to eating family suppers around the table and not from their hands in front of the television. Meals were said to bring everyone together in delicious harmony. Not the Millers. As a child he had used to dread eating with his parents, and in the holidays the exercise, as hated as detention, took place three times a day. His father would come home from the studio for lunch, walking into the kitchen at one o'clock and expecting Iona to put two courses on the table. Kit recalled with unforgiving clarity the gulp as Tod swallowed his food and the scrape of his knife on the plate. Kit was so nervous of having his head bitten off that he would clear his throat before asking, 'Please may I be excused?' Then he would be snapped at for clearing his throat.

Kit had loved the school canteen for its fried food, its noise and its chaos. He had loved tea at Rob's house after school, handed out in front of the television or self-served off the breakfast bar in their kitchen. As an adult he favoured portable food: he liked to stand in the street at night and eat a kebab, or buy an orange off a stall on Portobello Road and peel it there and then. But sitting down to a meal laid at a table filled him with tension and dread. He had always tried to avoid meals with girlfriends. 'Let's go to the pub,' he said to them, 'and if we're hungry, we can eat.'

'Look,' Alice might say, pointing at a restaurant as they walked through Soho. 'That looks nice. Can we stop? I'm starving.'

'Are you? I'm not hungry at all,' he would reply, and they would carry on walking.

When she was pregnant she had often had to eat alone. 'I feel like such a pig,' she had said, 'but I can't help it: this baby needs food.'

Kit knew that Alice had been brought up in a nice environment with united parents, a brother who was good at maths and, of course, the clear-sighted Emmy. Suppers at their house would have been, he guessed, like those at Rob's: noisy, and undertaken with great appetite. Appetite was frowned upon by Tod: it did not conform to his desired aesthetic.

But his father's own appetites, as Kit discovered later in life, had not been held in such restraint. They had had their freedoms, but in secrecy. It was that which made Kit angriest, even now: he and his mother had been confined by Tod's authority; his father's stamp had been on everything, right down to the teaspoons, *and all that*

time... the indulgence of Rosie. It was shocking. When
he had met Rosie, with her nail polish and her clattering
gold bangles, he had felt more betrayed by the kind of
relationship hers and Tod's had turned out to be –
expansive, vibrant and generous – than by the discovery
of an affair. It made a mockery of the constraints under
which he and his mother were made to live.

And yet: these revelations had not been enough to lead
him to pity his mother. Adolescence seemed to dispense
with sympathy, and he was disgusted by her instead. He
had remained so for quite some time. He still preferred to
regard her as incomplete.

With a speculative eye, he watched her finish making dinner. He threw his cigarette on to the fire when she pulled
the plates from the oven.

'Come on, Tod,' she called into the hall, 'we're
ready.'

Tod pushed his way into the room in his chair. His
eyes were bloodshot and his newly cut hair stood on end.
'What are we having?' he asked. 'Some vegetable nonsense?'

'Dear me, you are determined to be unpleasant, aren't
you?' said Iona, putting Tod's plate on the table. 'I've cut
it up, and there's mustard on the table if you want it.'

'You can hardly accuse *me* of being ungrateful,'
declared Tod, looking greedily at his plate, 'when *you*
refuse to accept my generous offer which, may I say, is
going to leave our son homeless.'

'Please don't pretend you've taken *my* wishes into any
sort of consideration,' said Kit in indignation.

With a satisfied air as if so far this evening things were going exactly according to plan, Tod pushed himself close to the table and unfolded his napkin on his knee. Picking up his fork, he ignored Kit and continued with his theme. 'Well, it doesn't matter, because I shall give the money to someone who will appreciate it. Someone who has *always* appreciated me.'

Kit, stepping forward to take his plate from his mother, saw with admiration that she was not going to take the bait. He wished he had been able to hold his own tongue. All his tightly wound thinking, he saw now, was years out of date. His mother could not be pierced by Tod, not tonight nor ever again.

Tod concentrated on his food for a minute, but as soon as he could speak he returned to his theme. Kit wondered why his father could not have become, in old age, more like Matisse and less like King Lear.

Tod had once said to him, 'All arguments are about either sex or money. If you look at them hard enough, they will always come down to one of those two things.'

Kit had found this to be true in life, although in his experience there was always the third option, that the argument could be spawned by a combination of the two. He anticipated such a discussion this evening: Tod had introduced two subjects, Rosie and the sale of his house, and then drawn his chair to the table as if to a ringside seat at the match.

But Iona did not want to argue and Kit could see that Tod was finding her passivity frustrating, like boxing against a cushion. Kit's habit was to put up his guard and defend himself as well as he could, but Iona was regarding her ex-husband with a reserve, a detached calm, that seemed to madden him. She had taken herself out of range. She answered him with cool politeness but she would not strike him back.

After dinner Iona murmured to Kit, 'He's worse than ever.' Now that Tod was asleep in front of the fire, hanging from his wheelchair like a monstrous bat, she seemed close to collapse.

'I know,' said Kit. 'I feel like dumping him in a hedge.'

Iona giggled. 'I'd rather you dumped him on an aeroplane, otherwise he might find his way back, like when you try to get rid of mice.'

Kit snorted. 'That's not how I get rid of mice,' he said with a growl. 'I poison 'em.'

'Oh, but that's a *town* mouse,' said Iona, looking up at him through her spectacles. 'That's quite a different thing. You wouldn't poison a dear little country mouse.'

Kit smiled inside and loved her, just for a moment. 'I can't help wondering why he insisted on coming here, instead of having his solicitor write you a letter?'

'I expect he wanted to see the look of pathetic gratitude on my face,' said Iona with a faint smile, 'which would explain why he's so cross. But honestly, Kit, what would I want with his money? It's a bit late for that sort of thing.'

Kit remembered his father saying, 'You can't write back; she's living in some hostel, some place for runaways,' when he came home from school and found a letter. 'I expect you could have done with it at one stage,' he remarked now.

'Oh well,' Iona shrugged. She turned a dishcloth on the surface of the table, 'It's all so long ago, now. I can't remember.' Then she straightened her back. 'Oh, Kit,' she sighed, 'I do so love seeing you! I know these circumstances are awful – tragic! – but I can't help it. And I adore your Alice! Poor thing, I wish she weren't so sad. Dreadful to feel as unhappy as that.' She shook her head. 'You must have been having an awful time.'

Kit thought it over: the folded body in the back of the car; the blood on the hotel bathroom floor; the slow footfall, up and down the basement stairs; her expressionless face looking up at him from the garden. 'Yes,' he said in despair. 'We have. I wish I knew what to do about it.'

'Don't do a thing, Sit tight, and be kind. You're a dear boy, Kit, though I know you'll hate me for saying so.'

Kit struggled before muttering gruffly, 'I don't hate you.'

'And now your soppy old mum is going to bed,' said Iona. She patted him on the sleeve before turning away. 'Put the guard on the fire before you go up, won't you?'

'What about Dad?'

'Oh, for Pete's sake, leave him. He doesn't deserve to be looked after.'

Kit lay down flat on the rug in front of the fire. Bones, next to him, thumped her tail on the floor. *Friends again.*

He blew smoke at the ceiling, drowsy with red wine and warmth, and wondered about it all. His thoughts moved at random through his mind, striking the surface now and again without purpose.

It occurred to him that when Tod had told him of his intention to sell the house he had reacted without doing any sort of inventory of his feelings. He had not asked himself, *Do I mind?* because he must: his father expected him to.

Iona had presented an alternative. She had rejected outright the role prescribed for her by Tod, and Kit was impressed. *Well I never*, he smiled to himself, *I am impressed by my mother.*

It upset him that his father had not considered him, but it should not have surprised him. It had always been the case; he had never been part of his father's plans. He could not – would not – go on being disappointed by Tod. It would be too stupid; too goldfish-like.

To resent your own child for taking its place in the world! To dispute, to inhibit, to resent, to punish – and all for vanity, for selfishness! *Please may I be excused.* His head was spinning. He thought of Alice, and of the lost baby. He remembered his shameful feelings, during her pregnancy. He sat up and looked into the fire, and Bones lifted her head to regard him with her steady gaze.

I never wanted it, he thought. *It was better that it died than had me as its father.*

He looked at Tod, snoring in his chair; he looked over his shoulder. He had a mad suspicion that someone in the room could read his mind. *Alice must never know,* he thought in desperation. But then, as he continued to sit and meet these teeming thoughts, a part of him wanted to scribble their message on the sky.

The next morning, in the hospital car park, Tod refused to get out of the car. Kit had to leave the engine running to keep him warm.

'I've got a plane to catch, don't forget,' Tod said as Kit opened the car door.

'There's plenty of time.'

'She'll be too tired to talk, she won't want you there,' continued Tod, pursing his lips. 'It's always a mistake to visit people in hospital, they don't like it –'

Kit shut the car door on him.

In the lift Kit examined his expression. *She's not dying,* he thought to himself. *You don't have to look so morbid.* He hesitated outside the ward, his trembling hand raised to push the swing doors, and then he propelled himself forward. On the other side of the door he met a fuggy smell that reminded him of a long-haul flight: reheated food and air that had been breathed over and over.

He found Alice, lying like a shadow in her bed. She had been awake, staring at the ceiling, and when Kit came in her eyes flicked towards him.

He knew from the moment he met her gaze that it was not going to be all right. For a moment, in the car on the way there, he had allowed himself to conceive a fantasy: that she would beckon him to her bedside with an outstretched hand, and that they would embrace. That she would have woken up the way she was before the crash. But she had not; her face was a bricked-up window.

'Hello,' he said in a timid whisper. 'How are you feeling?'

'Like an idiot. I can't believe they're not letting me go.

All I need is a decent night's sleep, and I'm not going to get one in here.'

'Mum says you can go to Trebartha, until you're well enough to go home.'

'Home? You mean, your house?'

Kit did not reply. She seemed to have got ahead of him in their conversation. He felt as if he were on the wrong page of the script, turning the pages only to get more and more lost.

'Where's your dad?' she asked.

'In the car. I'm taking him to Heathrow in a minute. And then…' he hesitated. 'What shall I do? Do you want me to come back?'

Now it was Alice's turn not to answer. Kit was unnerved. The knowledge was creeping up on him that this conversation was turning into *that* conversation. After a moment or two Alice said, 'Kit…' and did not go on.

'Is it over?' Kit said.

Alice turned on to her side towards him in the bed. She put her hands, palms together, under her head. 'Yes,' she said. It was too clean a shot not to take. 'It's over. It's been over since… oh, for ages. Maybe since the car fell off the mountain.'

Kit let the words fall into his mind. Somewhere on the ward a patient began calling, 'Nurse, nurse –' in a plaintive, tearful voice.

'We fucked it,' Kit murmured. 'And I still don't know how, or why. I thought… you might come back. The old you. But you –'

'I'm tired,' Alice interrupted him, her voice much louder than his. She shut her eyes. 'I don't want to talk about it – there's no point going over and over what happened. Everything's different, now.'

There was a pause. 'Don't worry, I get it,' he answered, as harshly as he could. 'I'm not going to try to change your mind.'

Relieved, Alice said, 'I'll get Emmy to collect my stuff. She can find a time that suits you.'

But Kit was not ready for Alice to be relieved. Even though he had anticipated the relationship ending, he was still shocked – as if he had been listening out for a gunshot, but could not help flinching when it came. He realised, all at once, that he was being dumped and he felt the cliff's edge under his shoe. He scrabbled for a foothold, saying, 'Christ', and then, 'Fuck', and rubbing his head. Something burned in his chest and he struggled to contain it. 'Fucking *hell*,' he went on, 'this is *shit*. Do you have *any idea* how impossible you've been? I've bent over backwards –'

'You don't have to, any more,' interrupted Alice, her voice cleared of expression. 'You might as well go.' The words hung weightless in the air, like smoke on a still afternoon. As if she were afraid of them, Alice said hurriedly, 'Anyway, I want to go back to sleep. I'm tired.'

She seemed to be holding illness up in front of herself like a screen, which made her position unarguable. Kit felt wrong-footed and confused: if she was the weak one, the one in bed, why did he feel so powerless? He got up, but then as he turned away Alice said, 'Kit', in quite a different voice, and he turned back to face her. 'Can I...' She swallowed. 'Can I keep Bones?'

You don't deserve an answer, Kit thought. 'I've left her with Mum for the time being,' he said.

Alice laughed, her voice as hard as a breaking twig. 'I get it.'

Kit said with indignation, 'Don't be like that. I'm not saying "no" I'm saying, 'Let's see what happens. You might feel different, when you're better.'

'Goodbye, Kit.'

When Kit got back into the car Tod said, 'I knew she wouldn't want you there for long.'

'Yes, you were right,' said Kit. He put the car into reverse and turned to see his way out of the space.

4

The next time Alice woke up Emmy was there, sitting in silence beside her, holding her hand.

In all the weeks and months since the Dead Sea Alice had not wept at all, but when she saw Emmy's weary face the tears came and she cried as if she would never stop. She almost choked.

'I'm sorry,' she said, 'I've been so stupid.'

'Don't be sorry for me,' Emmy said in reply, looking up. 'Be sorry for yourself.'

When she was able, Alice said, 'Where's Bones?'

'She's fine. She's with Iona.'

'Is she eating?'

Emmy smiled a half-smile at this. 'Yes, she's eating.'

'Can you stay?'

'For a bit. I've come to take you home.'

'Home to where?'

'To Iona's place,' said Emmy. 'For the moment. Is that OK?'

Alice did not ask, *Why not home to your flat?* She knew the answer: they did not trust her to be left alone.

Part Four

1

In London Kit rose each morning like a clockwork toy, feeling his way into his clothes and stumbling downstairs to the kitchen to begin his first and favourite ritual of the day: coffee. He had rules about coffee, and obeying those rules made him feel as if the day was going to go right.

It had to be made in the screw-down Bialetti. The coffee (Ethiopian) had to have been freshly ground. London water would not do in the chamber of the machine; it had to be bottled (Scottish). His coffee was drunk with milk before lunch, but without after, and it had to make his heart bounce like a ping-pong ball on a stone floor.

He had never considered himself to be a person who liked to live according to a strict programme of scheduled events, but during the time he had shared the house with Alice he had been brought face to face with the immutability of his own habits. For example, when she had moved in she had begun eating her muesli out of the very same bowl from which he preferred (in the French style) to drink his coffee. Sometimes, in the morning, when he had put his hand up to the usual place on the shelf, his bowl had not been there. He might then have discovered it in the sink, hosting a couple of squeezed-out teabags, or on a side table in the sitting room, or, worst of all, it might have been in the bathroom where Alice sometimes took it to finish eating while she dressed.

The point was that it might be neither clean nor on the shelf and this small absence had altered his morning in a way it had not been altered before Alice. He had felt a squeeze around his chest, for a brief moment, and then had looked for something else to use.

Kit liked his coffee from a cup which was lightweight, squat and without a handle. He despised mugs. Nothing would have induced him to use a mug. They reminded him of pottery – pottery wheels – craft – colourful knit-wear.

He had found a second-favourite coffee cup and had started to hide it in the cupboard where Alice would not see it, so there could be no second disappointment so early in the morning.

Now she had gone there would be no further domestic incidents of this type, but she had left a kind of watermark in his house and he found it hard not to be reminded of her. And then, to be reminded of her was harder still.

He heard the chuckle of the coffee coming through, and switched off the gas. The Bialetti would rest for a moment. The milk was heating in its pan, just beginning to bubble at its edges, and he switched off the gas underneath that too.

He looked out at the garden, in which nothing moved.

Since he had left Cornwall there had been further events, all quite beyond his control, which had combined to give Kit the feeling that he was a fish unexpectedly hoisted on deck, opening and shutting its mouth, soon to suffocate.

First, Emmy had come and taken away Alice's belongings (and Kit, knowing he was a coward, had stayed away until she had finished).

Second, builders had started work on the studio. Kit had arrived one morning and found a skip in the road containing everything that belonged to him. It was fair to say that he had been notified that this would happen, and on which day, but he had taken no notice. The studio was now a building site but soon would be a desirable residence boasting an interior designed by Tod Miller.

And third, the house had been sold. A young, professional couple had bought it, the sort Kit pictured drinking lattes in the afternoon. They were not English; they were smart, rich and unconcerned. 'We're trying to get pregnant,' the wife said to Kit. 'It's the right time.' Her husband was a banker – so was she, but she had stopped work for the moment. She wore smooth caramel clothes and had glossy hair that swung in a high ponytail. Kit lapped up everything about her, creating fantasies in which he tore the cashmere from her bosom. She had kissed her husband in the hall when the agent was turning out the kitchen lights, and Kit had spied on them from the top of the stairs.

She was going to gut the place. Architects, builders,

interior designers and decorators arrived in a continuous stream, or so it felt to Kit. They had asked if he minded, but Kit did not mind anything at the moment. He would not have noticed if they had run a bulldozer through the sitting room.

His father's possessions – which made up most of the contents of the house – were removed by a team of Spanish removal men, and Kit put his own belongings (but for the coffee pot and the goldfish) into a hired Transit van and drove them out of London and into Kent where he had rented a unit in a self-storage centre based on an industrial estate off the M25.

It was a hot day, much hotter than usual for the time of year. Kit drove with the windows open and enjoyed posing as a van driver: cigarette stuck between his fingers and the radio on loud. He turned into the industrial estate and paused beside a map which showed the location of each business. He leaned out of the window to see where Core Storage was situated and noticed that the roads were named after what must have been here before the concrete: Willow Grove; Bushy Way; Reed Lane. The map, he thought to himself, was a memorial of the sacrifices made by nature for light industry.

Core Storage was furthest away from the road and although there were no willows now it did feel haunted by those felled trees. It was quiet and calm, and the noise of the motorway was smothered by the sound of a stream which had been channelled into a concrete ditch.

A huge metal warehouse stood like an ocean liner in a dazzling sea of white concrete, and in front of it, ugly and squat as a tug, was a prefab unit with caged windows and 'Reception' written over the door. Kit climbed the steps and pushed open the door. Inside, it smelled of a thousand packets of crisps.

A young man sitting behind the desk dragged his eyes away from his laptop when Kit walked in. He did not change his expression when he looked at Kit and this gave Kit the feeling that something vile and frightening had been taking place on the computer screen.

The man printed off forms for Kit to fill in and then sold him a padlock – since he had forgotten to bring one – at an exorbitant price. Armed with this and dragging a huge metal trolley bearing the first load of his possessions, Kit went in search of his unit.

The white glare on the concrete outside made the inside of the shed seem black and cold as a lake. Kit had to travel up to the third floor in a goods lift that needed its grilled doors shutting in a strict sequence. Then he wandered down long corridors, strip lights flickering on and off overhead as he passed them and his trolley clanking behind him. He felt as if he and his luggage were starting a life sentence in a maximum security prison.

The space was vast and confusing, one yellow door after another, each bearing a number. At the end of a row a new series of numbers would start which seemed to have nothing to do with those which had come before.

One unit door stood open and Kit looked in as he drew alongside. Inside the cell, a man was leafing through a box of papers, one of many hundred, stacked up to the ceiling around him. He looked up at Kit, eyes wide, and they stared at each other for a second until Kit had passed. Kit felt as if he had caught the man undressing; these burrows were private. He resolved that the next open door he passed, he would not turn his head, but the temptation was too great and this time he saw a middle-aged woman unwrapping teacups from sheets of newspaper. A baby's carrycot stood beside her on top of a box.

When he found number 333, he pulled open the door and stared into an empty grey chamber. He pulled his trolley in to unload it, and then went rattling back down the long corridors to his van.

It took him four journeys, and it was a chore, but nothing more than that. He waited to feel sad or upset, but none of this seemed to have much to do with him. After all, in every unit, stretching away from him in every direction, was the same collection of belongings.

When he had locked the door with his new padlock, he returned to his empty van and got his cigarettes out of the front. In the reception was a drinks machine and, holding his breath, he went in and got a can of Coke. The young man regarded him in silence.

Back outside, Kit found a sliver of grass beside the concrete riverbank. He sat down on it to smoke.

He could not help but think of Jordan: this was what he had been doing while Karim had climbed the hill for help. That behaviour seemed so peculiar when he thought about it now. He had told everyone, afterwards, 'I think I must have been in shock.' But he knew that he had not been. He had been propelled by fear, not shock. He had run away. It had seemed at the time that there was nothing else to be done. He had been too frightened to stay with Alice.

What did it matter? Nothing he had done would have made any difference to the outcome: the baby had died; Alice was gone.

He lay on the grass under the baking sun and imagined what he might do with his new life. Perhaps a train to Paris and on to Nice, to Genoa, to Naples and still further south. An apartment in Sicily; painting outdoors; evenings in the village square; local wine and local girls.

Almost in the same moment he realised that his passport was still tucked in the bag he had taken to Jordan, and that the bag was locked in the depths of his locker. *Oh well,* he thought, stubbing out the cigarette. *So much for that.* He turned to chuck the butt in the stream but stopped himself and dropped it into the Coke can instead. He squashed the can flat with his fist and carried it back to his van.

On the way back into London he stopped on the King's Road and bought a new coffee cup.

'Would you like to see the Tod Miller range?' the assistant asked.

'No, I would not,' Kit replied. 'I would like to see the normal person's range.'

That night he wandered around the house, going from one empty room to another. He had an uncertain feeling, as if he'd missed a step in the dark. It was not the emptiness of the building that was strange, it was the absence of meaning. He longed for resonance.

He looked at the pale patches on the walls and the scuffs and stains on the floor and called to mind which picture or piece of furniture had been there, but the images were faint. Like the Cheshire Cat, these marks were the traces of an expression where once there had been a meaningful body. Blue dust circled in greasy clumps around his feet.

When he climbed the stairs he stroked the flat of his hand along the wall in a gesture of sympathy: *Poor house, there, there*. He felt a kind of kinship.

In the basement there was nothing of Alice's left but a bottle of scent on the shelf in the bathroom. Kit scratched his stomach and stared at the bevelled glass, his mind empty of thoughts. Then he picked the bottle up and sprayed some scent into the air. Closing his eyes, he inhaled.

He felt his mind's eye open like a door in a garden wall and through it he saw Alice sitting beside him on a bench outside the pub, the second time they had met. He remembered kissing her, her laughing face turned towards him, self-conscious but as open and guileless as a picture book.

They had sat outside drinking rounds of Guinness and whisky. When the eleven o'clock bell rang Kit took Alice's whisky glass away from her and kissed her smiling mouth. He had felt her light, shallow breath on his upper lip between kisses, and he had inhaled her scent, the same as the one he inhaled now and as much a part of her attraction as her smile, or her warm skin, or her tangle of dark hair.

Now, in the cold, dejected bathroom, she was brought back to him only in the sense that when he opened his eyes he felt more lonely than he ever had in his life. That girl had gone, and the Kit who had kissed her that night had gone too.

2

Packing for her trip to Florida, back in the winter, Alice had thought, *I bet it comes on the plane. That would be absolutely* typical. She had put a packet of Tampax, and another of Nurofen Plus, into her hand luggage. But – and at the time she had been thankful – it had not.

Once in her parents' apartment, waking in their spare room, she had scanned her pyjamas every morning for the tell-tale spots. After a few days the relief that she had not marked the sheets gave way to concern. Finally she had begun to go cold when she woke and found nothing: 'Please, please, please,' she had muttered under her breath, sitting on the loo and squeezing at her tummy as if it were a sponge and she could wring it out.

On her last night she had lain awake – a white night, Kit called it – listening to the slap of water against the pontoon. She knew she could not put off going to the chemist any longer.

'The service takes an hour,' her father said, leaning in through the car window when she dropped them off at their church. 'An hour... or so. We'll wait for you here.'

'Oh, *Robert*,' Alice's mother rebuked him, still in the back seat, rummaging for tissues in her handbag. 'You know perfectly well it's an hour and twenty minutes.' She rolled her eyes at Alice in the rear-view mirror. 'He's only saying that to make sure you're back on time.'

'I will be,' Alice reassured her.

'Come on, Carol,' Robert said, checking his watch.

Alice's mother, still sitting in the back seat of the car, snapped her bag shut and said to Alice, 'Are you sure you don't want to come?'

I'd rather stick my head in a blender, thought Alice, but she turned, smiling, and replied, 'No thanks, Mum – maybe next time. I'll see you in a bit.'

'Well,' Carol said, opening the car door, 'I'll say a little prayer for you, and afterwards we'll all have a nice lunch. We needn't leave for the airport until four.'

Alice watched her parents reach for each other's hands as they walked towards the building. 'Jesus Loves a Sinner', read the sign outside. When her mother and father had gone through the glass doors, Alice put the car into drive and pulled away from the kerb.

It irritated Emmy that their parents had become churchgoers now that they lived in Florida. 'But we went to church at home,' Alice said, sticking up for them, during one of Emmy's rants.

'No we didn't,' said Emmy. 'Only at Christmas. We had that beautiful church at the end of the garden, the perfect little English church, and we went inside it once a year. And now they go to some fucking drive-through church with electric guitars and morons waving their arms. It's nothing to do with God; they just do it because they're bored and lonely.'

'Isn't that why everyone goes to church?'

'Oh *God*,' said Emmy in frustration. 'Stop defending them! You know what I mean.'

Emmy was enraged further when her mother said, 'It's a good way to meet people.'

'You don't even pretend to be religious,' accused Emmy.

'Church is more than religion,' said Carol in a mild, rehearsed voice. 'And religion is more than church.'

'That's just the kind of useless platitude they come up with in those places,' spat Emmy.

'Why are you so mean to Mum?' Alice asked her sister afterwards. 'You never used to be.'

'I don't know,' Emmy admitted. 'I can't seem to help myself. It's why I don't go there any more. It makes me vile and I hate myself. I can just about be civil to them once a year, in London, but *that place*. It kills me. And they're so stupid now, it makes me sad.'

'You can't miss it,' Alice's mother had said of the chemist's shop. 'No one could.' Alice pulled off the freeway and into the retail park and yes, there it was: a colossal brown shed squatting between Chicken Shack and Brett's

Discount Electricals in the midst of an archipelago of superstores which floated on a lagoon of black tarmac. Huge letters spelled out Drug Barn, and underneath, Your Family's Pharmaceutical Superstore.

'But what is it you need?' her mother had asked. 'I've got aspirin and things, here.'

Alice had anticipated this question. 'Tampax,' she had lied smoothly.

Carol had clicked her tongue and said, 'Probably the only thing I don't have.' Her voice had almost been wistful.

Alice parked her parents' car next to a tiny tree that had been secured upright and ringfenced with a steel cage as if it might otherwise have tried to run away to a forest somewhere, in search of a better life. Alice looked at it, sitting in the car with the engine switched off. This was the first moment of solitude she had spent, she realised, since coming to stay with her parents.

She felt sorrow and pity for everything today, as if she had been stripped of a layer of skin: this tree; the flies that beat on her parents' screen door; the Mexican gardener pointing his leaf blower dejectedly at the ground. Even the sight of the clock, perched on the 'barn' in front of her and made to resemble an English stable clock, brought a pungent wash of homesickness.

Or perhaps this is morning sickness, she thought in dread. *Not necessarily, no*, she told herself. *Don't panic.* She had only started to feel sick when she thought she might be pregnant, not the other way round. This 'about-to-take-a-driving-test' feeling might be nerves.

The shop was as cold as a morgue. There was music playing: Drug Barn Radio. Alice's head swam. How reassuring could Celine Dion be, Alice wondered, to people who were really ill? She supposed its purpose was to subdue, like in a lift or before the plane took off.

Aisle after aisle stretched away from her, rows of bottles and jars forming blocks of colour. Lights shone from above and a polished floor gleamed beneath her feet. She slid along each aisle like a figure skater, reading the brand names of medicines, toothpastes and shampoos she did not recognise. Hidden away in a corner, like New Zealand on the atlas, was a section marked 'Feminine Products'. *The corner of shame,* Alice thought.

It occurred to her then, as she stared at the Drug Barn 2-4-1 Pregnancy Test Kit, that it might not even be legal to be pregnant and unmarried in Florida. America was so odd. She imagined, as she did a hundred times a day, what Kit would say if he were here. Then, *Kit,* she thought, *oh God,* and fear lifted her up by the scruff.

The woman at the till, Emmy's age, was heavily pregnant. As she passed the test kit over the scanner she smiled at it, and at Alice when she took her twenty-dollar bill.

'Good luck, honey,' she said.

Alice blushed. 'Thank you. Good luck with your… the birth.'

'It's my fourth,' said the woman, putting one hand on her stomach. 'My husband says after this one he's gonna tie up *his* toobs, an' then he's gonna tie up *my* toobs.' She laughed, a series of delighted squeaks, like a toy being sat on.

On the other side of the automatic doors the hot, damp air caught Alice unawares, as it always seemed to. She had been here for a week – and she had come many times before – but she never seemed to get used to the air. Walking outside, here, was not like walking into fresh air, it was like entering the changing rooms at a public swimming pool: fuggy, hot and smelling of disinfectant. Inside was chilling with the atmosphere sapped cold, dry and colourless by air-conditioning.

In the Chicken Shack she sat at a window table and drank Diet Coke until she needed to have a pee. *Fuck, fuck, fuck*, she thought. It was nearly time to go back to the church. She got up and dragged herself towards the door marked 'Restrooms'.

On the wall of the cubicle someone had written *I hate God*. As Alice sat and waited, the plastic wand in her hand, she thought of the tears that had been shed in this cubicle, in this Ladies' loo, in the Chicken Shack, next to the Drug Barn; the acres of tarmac outside; the lonely little trees separated from each other by iron bars; the cars speeding by on the highway; the dead animals pasted on to the road's surface. She stared down at the white stick. Nothing yet. Leaning her head on the cubicle wall, she waited.

This visit had not been a success. For the first time, Alice felt impatient; restless; frustrated by her parents' bovine languor. She knew now what kept Emmy away because her feelings were similarly mixed. Something had changed.

Perhaps it was having Kit, her first real boyfriend,

waiting – she hoped! – back in London. She seemed to see everything through his eyes and it made her dissatisfied, as he would have been. She knew she could never bring him here.

Kit had a habit of calling Alice's father Nigel, rather than Robert. At first it had amused Alice, then it stung her. 'Why can't you remember his name?' she asked.

'I don't know,' said Kit. 'He just seems like a Nigel.'

'But you've never met him.'

'I know, but I have such a clear picture, in my mind.'

She had been shocked by how much she had hated leaving Kit. It had made her fearful: not just afraid to leave him but nervous of that fear, and of the power it held. It brought home to her an inequality she had suspected, that she did not mean to him what he meant to her. It made her tremble to think that if she wasn't with him she slid out of his mind. 'I'll ring you,' she had said to him, hugging him goodbye.

'Yes, do,' Kit had replied, kissing the top of her head and smoothing her hair behind her ears. 'Although – not too much. We don't want to end up having those dreary conversations about the weather.'

Emmy had tried to reassure her on the way to the airport. 'It's his age,' she had said. 'He's had lots of relationships, and you haven't. You're bound to mind more. And anyway, he's a man, which explains everything, and on top of that he's a painter and they never think about much except painting – in the rare moments,' she had added, 'that they aren't thinking about themselves.'

'Oh,' Alice had said in disappointment. 'So shouldn't I phone him, then?'

'Yes, do,' Emmy had answered, relenting a little. Then

she had echoed Kit, 'But not too much.'

To her parents, Alice was still a child and she had used to find it easy to play that part when she visited, like putting on the pyjamas her mother laid out for her on her pillow in the apartment's spare bedroom. Mrs Fox, her old stuffed toy, would be there on the pillow too, and on the kitchen table at breakfast there would be chocolate spread.

But this time, 'Is there any honey?' she had asked at breakfast.

'Honey?' her mother had said in surprise. 'But you like chocolate spread.'

After a few days Alice was restless and suggested she might hire a car. 'But why would you?' her mother had responded, puzzled and hurt. 'We'll do everything together.'

'Driving in the States is no joke,' said her father, putting his spectacles down on the table. 'I wouldn't like you to risk it.'

'But Dad,' remonstrated Alice, standing on one leg. 'I passed my test years ago. I've driven all over Europe.'

'It's not the same,' said Robert in a firm voice.

'Listen,' said Emmy, on the telephone, 'it's because they feel guilty about selling up and fucking off to Florida when you were still a kid – as well they might. You were a child when they left, and that's the person they picture when they think of you. And it will be, until something radical happens.'

This new Alice, Kit's girlfriend, seemed reluctant to

give way to the little girl just for the sake of her parents' quietude. The new Alice dominated still, even though Kit was far away.

How could it be hard to be submissive? The dilemma puzzled her. She wanted so much to be peaceable but she felt as if her identity was being divided, again and again, like a cake into pieces. One for Emmy, one for Kit, one for her parents.

But if she were pregnant, she thought now, that would take the whole cake: *mother.*

Her friends at school had used to say, 'You're lucky, your parents are in love, they're so sweet together', and Alice would agree, but in private she felt dubious. Robert and Carol were, to Alice, a sealed unit. When the three of them had watched television together, not on school nights but at the weekends, her parents would sit tucked together on the sofa. Alice would sit in the armchair, with Mrs Fox. She would keep her eyes on the screen when she heard her parents' intermittent kisses.

Why could she not have been more like Emmy, who would say, 'Ugh, gross, you guys make me puke', and chuck a pillow at their heads? Alice would stay motionless, and go hot with blushing.

'The trouble with being a mum,' Carol said once in exasperation, when Emmy had been sent home again and her parents were wondering what to do, 'is it goes on such a bloody long time. It's interminable.'

It is, reflected Alice now, *unless you move abroad, to a place your children don't want to visit.* Children usually moved away from their parents, didn't they? Look at Emmy: 'Fuck you both, I'm going to London', and she had swung out of the door with her canvas bag.

But when it came to Alice's turn it had been Robert and Carol who had come up with the plan of escape, digging their tunnel in the dead of night to get away from washing Alice's games kit and listening to her practise her arpeggios. 'We'll be near Pete and his girls,' her mother had said to her, announcing the emigration.

But I'm your *girl*, Alice had thought.

Her time was up: she only had to look down to see the result. She closed her eyes, inhaled and shut her mouth tightly. The air ballooned inside her.

All at once, with the plummeting clarity of a stone dropped into deep water, she knew – sitting there on the Chicken Shack toilet seat – that the stick in her hands would only confirm, in blue and white stripes, what she was already certain of: she was pregnant. Of course she was – how could she ever have doubted it? Her mind dipped and darted like a swallow searching the sky, as it had been doing all week as the days had gone by and the curse – not a curse, a longed-for blessing! – had not come.

She thought of Kit, crossed the fingers of one hand, raised the baton with the other and opened her eyes.

3

'Oh look,' said Rob, checking his emails while Charlotte packed her school bag, 'Kit's throwing a party.'

'Christ, men are predictable,' said Naomi. She was slumped at the kitchen table, waiting for her period and not in a good mood. 'I expect he'll seduce some poor teenager.'

Rob rang Kit to say yes, they would come.

'I'm going to get pissed,' Kit said to him, 'and shag someone young and unsuitable.'

'You lucky bastard,' sighed Rob. 'That's exactly what I feel like doing.' Instead, he had decided he would get high. 'I'm going to buy some super-strong pot,' he said to Naomi with defiance.

'Pathetic,' said Naomi.

The man who delivered the pot sold Rob a gram of MDMA and Rob wrapped a pinch of it in a screw of

Rizla paper, for Kit to swallow.

'It's a present,' said Rob, 'to remind you of the old days.'

Kit examined the little paper nugget as if it were a treasure from a lost civilisation.

'My God,' he said in a whisper, 'Ecstasy! I'm being transported back to my youth – I feel like Proust and that little bun. I can't believe anyone makes MDMA any more. Don't all kids take Ketamine these days? That's what I read in the *Observer*.'

'Someone will always make Ecstasy,' pronounced Rob.

The party was going to be a success, Kit could tell. He was a good host – he had used to throw parties all the time. Now he wondered why he had ever stopped.

Since he had shut his belongings away in self-storage Kit had felt much better: cleaner, lighter, more flexible. He was relieved to be without Alice, to be losing the house, and even to have given up the dog. He was free! He could do anything: tonight, for example, he might do anything. He could get drunk, he could get high, he could get laid.

As he climbed the stairs to fetch more cigarettes, a pretty girl, leaning back on the banisters and shaking the ice cubes around her empty glass, said, 'Hello, Kit.' Kit smiled at her in return, feeling the thrill of promise. As he continued on his way he repeated his mantra to himself: *I'm going to get pissed, I'm going to get high and I'm going to get laid.*

He stopped on the landing and stared through the

window and down into the garden. Fingering the nugget of Ecstasy in his pocket he wondered whether to take it right away. He was surprised by a sudden wave of weariness and lassitude. This freedom did not *comfort* him, he realised in a horrible rush, it made him feel isolated. At present he was taking a kind of grim pleasure in isolation, but it would not last, and soon he would be lonely. He had always considered himself above loneliness – that it was for feeble, needy characters to feel lonely, and not for him – but now he felt a nudge of self-pity. With haste, as an incoming wave ploughs over the smaller ones before it, he erased these thoughts with another: *I need a drink.*

He collected the cigarettes and went back down to the basement (*I'm going to get pissed, I'm going to get high and I'm going to get laid,*) to stand close to the bar and drink three tequilas, swallowing the little paper parcel with his first and already beginning to feel its effects – a warming from the inside, the thrilling tremble of sensation – as he drank the last.

Kit didn't dance – he never did, it was one of his rules, like not wearing hats that came out of Christmas crackers – but he enjoyed watching others dance, particularly when he was getting high. He leaned on the door frame where one of the French windows stood open, half of him chilled by the outdoors and the other half stifled by the heat of the dance floor.

This had been Alice's bedroom. Now a trio of leggy, laughing girls, waving their arms above their heads, danced together where her bed had stood. With their long hair and limbs they swayed like reeds in a current. They all wore layers of gauzy cotton vests over tiny shorts, and Kit's impression was that none of them had quite finished getting dressed. He gazed at them in satisfaction. Who were these delightful girls?

Now, at last, everything felt pleasant and the complications of memory and experience were suspended. Kit drank some more tequila, thinking how delicious it was, and how positive he felt about drinking alcohol of any kind. Drinking was *good*. The music was *fantastic*.

Wanting his rush to develop without disturbance, he ducked out of the door and into the garden, weaving across the grass to the end furthest from the house.

In the damp shadow of the laurels, alone, he listened to the *thud-thud* of the music and felt it pulse in his chest. He noted the emerging response of his body to the pinch of powder he had swallowed, his sensations rising like fish to crumbs scattered on a pool of water. All in a moment he felt everything expand, both within and without him: 'Holy shit,' he laughed, staggering on his feet and stretching out his arms, 'I'm off my head.'

This was the spot where, as little boys, he and Rob had had their camp, sitting on the ground and making plans for world domination. When it rained they had heard the patter on those shining green leaves, but had stayed dry. It was like being in a jungle – or so they had imagined. 'Who shall we be today?' he had used to ask Rob, when they came out from the house. They had stopped being shot-down pilots or escaped prisoners only when lunch or tea had been called.

Remembering, Kit stared up at the sky, a thick, orange fug which seemed to press down on the roofs of the houses around him. The whole city was being smothered. No stars, no space rockets, no jungle, no shot-down parachutists. *Who shall we be today?*

He giggled: *I am high.*

Back in the house he found Rob on the dance floor, his hair and shirt darkened by sweat. His pupils looked like wet pebbles as he leaned towards Kit to shout, 'I think this E is deadly.'

Kit nodded his head up and down and noticed the whole room jolt. 'I'm twatted,' he replied. Rob laughed and clapped him on the shoulder, and then went back to dancing, one hand holding a bottle of beer, the other waving in the air. The smiling young girls danced round him.

Kit turned to see Naomi with her friend Gemma. They were watching Rob. 'I love my husband,' said Naomi, 'don't I?' She turned to Kit. 'You remember Gemma?'

'Sure,' shouted Kit. 'Hi Gemma.' He grinned at her. 'How are you?'

'I'm OK, thanks,' said Gemma. 'Great party. But then, you always did throw great parties.'

'I don't know why I stopped. What are you up to these days?'

'Oh, you know,' said Gemma, taking a swig from her beer bottle. 'Getting divorced.'

'That's great,' said Kit, not listening. 'Hey, Naomi, who are all those gorgeous girls hanging round your husband?'

Naomi laughed, and Gemma looked at him for a moment. 'One of them is my daughter,' she said in a cool voice.

'Yes, Kit,' laughed Naomi, 'you're so old that some of your friends have daughters you want to shag.'

'Ugh,' grimaced Gemma. 'Don't joke about it, it makes me feel sick. I'm going to get another drink.' She turned away.

'Well done,' said Naomi to Kit with heavy sarcasm. 'That Miller charm working its magic again.'

But Kit was so high he could not register what she said – it was as much as he could do to nod his delicate head, a bowl of water balanced on a shelf.

One of the girls tiptoed towards him, flamingo-like, and asked for a light. When he held out the flame she pulled her long hair out of its reach and bent over. Kit saw the neon nail polish flash at her fingertips and he stared at the smooth brown skin between her shoulder-blades. As she stood up again the strap of her vest fell down her arm, and she hitched it up before raising her lit cigarette to him in thanks. Kit was mesmerised.

'Thanks,' she said into his ear, raising her cigarette to him and sashaying back on to the dance floor.

'Close your mouth, Kit,' said Naomi. 'That was Caitlin.'

'Caitlin!' Kit flinched. 'Caitlin? Bloody hell.' She was Rob's stepsister, born when Rob and Kit had been teenagers. Kit remembered how much they had hated having a baby around. They wanted to lie in the garden and smoke dope, and Rob's mother had seemed always to be there, breastfeeding. 'It's totally revolting,' Rob had said in disgust. 'One, she's my mum, and two, she's too old to have a baby. It's embarrassing.'

And now here was Caitlin, all grown up. 'I wish you hadn't told me that,' he said to Naomi.

'And I wish you weren't such a perve,' responded Naomi. 'I'm going to the bar.'

The next time Caitlin walked past him, Kit said, 'I can't believe it's you.'

'I thought you hadn't recognised me!'

'Of course I do. Even without the P.E. kit.'

'Oh my God!' exclaimed Caitlin. 'That's right: you came to sports day; I won the high jump.' She teased him: 'Does that make you feel old?'

'Yes,' he confessed, 'but that's probably a good thing. To be reminded that time is short.' *This flirting*, he thought to himself, *is going to get me into bed with this unbelievable girl.*

Caitlin looked at him in a considering way for a moment. 'D'you want to go upstairs for a bit?' she asked him. 'It's too hot in here.'

They sat on the stairs above the packed hallway, passing a cigarette between them. 'This is a cool house,' Caitlin said. 'And a great party.'

'Thanks. Us old-timers know a thing or two about parties.'

'You're not *that* old,' said Caitlin. 'What are you, forty?'

'Not quite,' winced Kit. 'But I feel it.'

'My mum says it's having kids that ages you.'

Kit thought about this. It sounded so sad, it almost took the edge off his buzz. 'I expect she's right,' he said.

Caitlin dropped the cigarette end into her empty beer bottle and leaned towards Kit, pressing his shoulder with her own. At the same time she put one of her bare, neon-tipped feet alongside his, so that they were touching. She said, 'I had such a crush on you, when I was a kid.'

I'm drunk; I'm high; I'm about to get laid, thought Kit.

4

Iona found Alice in the caravan. It was a warm day. The door stood open and Alice was on her hands and knees scrubbing the floor, wearing yellow rubber gloves and with her hair, longer now, tied up in a red scarf. 'Hello,' she said, looking up. 'Have you come for a tour?'

But Iona could give only a faint smile. 'Such an odd thing,' she said with some hesitation, hovering on the bottom step. 'That was Kit on the phone. Says he's just passing Launceston. On his way here.'

Alice looked up from her bucket and scrubbing brush. 'Here? Kit? What do you mean?'

'That's what he said. He sounded… a bit odd. I couldn't tell, it was a bad line. I think he was driving.'

Alice sat back on her heels and rubbed a hand over her face, thinking, *Shit*.

The teardrop-shaped caravan had become her project

when she had decided not to go back to London with Emmy but to stay here with Iona for 'a bit'. It was nearly done: after the scrubbing she would paint it inside and then move in the furniture that she had found in the attic.

She had borrowed Jory from the garden for a couple of days' work and he had done the heavy chores, making the van watertight and ripping out the mildewed interior. Alice had found a sink in one of the sheds and Jory had plumbed it in for her. Then she had painted the outside a dark, glossy green and now it glowed like a lump of kryptonite in the corner of the field, giving her a satisfied feeling when she caught a glimpse of it from her bedroom window.

She wanted to live in it, perhaps for ever. Iona laughed when Alice said so, but Alice was serious. The thought of London, of a job and a flat, gave her hot and cold prickles. She did not like to think about that life for long. 'When are you coming back?' Emmy asked on the telephone. 'All your stuff is here. I've got your room ready.'

'Soon,' lied Alice. 'Definitely soon.'

In the beginning she had thought Kit might make contact, but he had not. Initially her thoughts had dwelled on him, then they paid him briefer visits. Soon he occurred to her only once in a while, and now it had begun to surprise her when Iona spoke of him, as she did sometimes: 'I wonder how poor Kit is,' she would say. 'I wish he'd get in touch.' The expression made Alice smile – *That will take more than a phone call*, she thought.

Here Alice was cocooned: no one knew her; she had no

past; anyone who asked was told that she was a friend of Iona's son, recovering from an illness. At first she had hated that tag, but now she had got used to it. Sometimes it was useful, excusing her of unpleasant duties.

This was unpleasant: Kit arriving out of the blue. Alice said, 'I can't... see him. I *can't.*'

But Iona was not listening, she was thinking of her son. Her son! How she loved him! And he was coming to visit, of his own accord. 'He'll be here in a minute,' she said. 'I hope he's all right. So unlike him, to do something spontaneous. I'd better make up a bed. And we must think of something nice to eat.' She turned back towards the house.

Alice thought, *What about me?* She peeled off her rubber gloves, dropped them on the floor in front of her and got to her feet.

Outside, Bones lay stretched out on the grass in the sun. Alice lay down beside her and, reaching out a hand, laid it on the dog's rough coat. 'Perhaps he's coming to take you away,' she said. Bones thumped her tail.

One night after the hospital she had woken in the dark and tried to identify the strong physical feeling that had woken her up. It was painful but familiar; a question she knew the answer to. Then she had realised: *I'm hungry.* She had slid out of bed and on to her feet, holding the bedstead with one hand, to see how steady her legs were.

Shuffling to the door, she had opened it and peered out. On the landing a light glowed under a pale shade. She had crept downstairs, one hand on the banister, shivering in her leggings and sweater, woollen socks snagging on the floorboards.

Iona's kitchen was warm and Alice had been drawn towards the Aga as if by a magnet. She knew what she wanted: *toast*. In the bread bin there was a chestnut-coloured loaf and Alice held it to her nose and took a deep breath. It smelled of rainy summer picnics.

She cut two pieces of bread, snared them in the Aga toaster, and put that under the lid on the hot plate. Then she waited, curling and uncurling her toes on the kitchen floor.

When she could smell the toast she removed it from the clinging embrace of the wire tongs and held a piece in each hand. Without pause or examination, she lifted one and took a bite. The crust crunched; the soft middle squished against the roof of her mouth; she tugged at the caramel interior with her teeth; heat burst in her face; the sharp smell filled up her nose and sparked tears to her eyes. Holding both pieces, eating one as she went, she had climbed the stairs back up to bed.

In the morning it had felt like a dream but she had found crumbs in the bed. *Begin again, every day*, she had been told. *Don't punish yourself for yesterday.*

Lying on the grass, she wished she had been given instructions for this occasion: the arrival of Kit. A month ago she would have taken Bones and hidden until he had gone, but now she pulled a polo-neck over her head and examined her face in the mirror screwed to the back of the caravan door, puffing out her cheeks in caricature.

She had learned not to look too long at her face, or to stare in the mirror in the bathroom when she got out of the bath. She wanted to feel better, so she ate. It made perfect sense. That was what she said to herself when she picked up her knife and fork.

When Alice had asked Iona if she could stay for a little bit longer, Iona had said, 'Only if you want to get better.'

Alice had flushed. 'I do,' she said.

'All right then. I want you to stay. But it means breakfast and dinner with me, and lunch with the students. Every day.'

'OK, fine.'

'And no long walks.'

Alice had agreed to everything, and she had kept her word. She was frightened of being sent away.

And so her body was changing – it could not be helped when Iona and the students ate like kings. After lunch the students went back to class – to the kitchen or the garden – and Alice washed and tidied up after them and drank a double espresso she made for herself using the Gaggia in the cookery school canteen. Professional-strength espresso gave her almost the same feeling she had used to get from skipping meals.

She sat on the step and untangled the gold hoops in her ears from her polo-neck. One of the things she had begun to do again was adorn herself: necklaces, earrings and make-up. Iona had lent her colourful sweaters and scarves.

One wet afternoon they had gone through Iona's wardrobe. 'Wow,' Alice had said, fingering the long sleeves of a silk dress. 'Look at all these!'

'Too good to wear,' sighed Iona. 'I should sell them.'

'Were you given them? For modelling?'

'No! God no, we weren't given anything. It was all quite different – models weren't revered, then. Unless you were Twiggy, I suppose. To my parents being a model was much worse than being a secretary – as far as they were concerned I was a fallen woman from the moment I took my first job. They were convinced I would be pregnant in about five seconds flat. As it turned out, they were absolutely right!' She laughed. 'Poor things. My father aged about a decade overnight when I told him, and another when he actually *met* Tod. They were the same generation, you see, which made it even worse. Their backgrounds could not have been more different: my father was terrified of him; thought he was both common and an artist: what could be worse? And yet he was desperate for Tod to marry me – that was all that mattered. Can you imagine?' She shook her head, straightening a dress on its hanger.

'But it wasn't the fifties, or the sixties,' said Alice. 'It was seventy something, wasn't it?'

'Only just. My parents came from Perthshire – it might as well have been the 1870s. It would still be the same now for people like them, I expect. Oh, Alice, I can't tell you how silly it all was! What a fuss… Thank God for dear little Kit. When he arrived, I wasn't so lonely, at least…' she broke off, smoothing the dresses back into line on their rail. 'Anyway, the answer to your question is no, I wasn't given them for modelling – I was given them by Tod. He was always very concerned with the way I looked. The funny thing was,' she mused, 'that it never felt like being given something; more like having something taken away.' Then she shut the cupboard door and did not say any more.

Alice was still able to appreciate the novelty of sitting still like this, and being content. She did not feel her failures crowding her back on to her feet, as she had used to in London. After the miscarriage each of her thoughts had been examined, questioned and investigated. How exhausting it had been, to live under her own, despotic rule! But now, while she fiddled with her caravan, or sat here on the step, her thoughts passed quite naturally through her head.

She wondered what Kit would make of her now. And what would she make of him?

Estrangement was an odd thing. It did not seem to have much to do with solitariness, or physical distance: she had felt most separate from Kit when she had lived in his house, and seen him every day. Then, she had wanted to put as much distance between them as she could.

At that time she had sometimes felt as if she had already disappeared, and that she might have overheard Kit on the telephone, saying to someone, 'Alice? No, I don't know what happened to her. She vanished.'

From the step she heard a familiar yet surprising sound: the slow clatter of a London taxi. Alice got up and walked back across the garden to the gravel to see a black cab waiting there. Alice could not help smiling as its engine was turned off and Kit emerged from the back as if he were getting out at home in London.

'Hello, Kit,' she said.

Kit looked at her. He seemed surprised to see her. 'Oh, yes, that's right.' He rubbed a hand over his head. 'OK here?' he said to the driver.

'You carry on, mate,' came the reply from the cab. 'Take your time.'

'It's all right,' said Kit to Alice. 'He's switched the meter off. We agreed a price.'

'I see.' She was trying to gauge Kit's mood. He seemed owlish; opaque. He was wearing last night's clothes – she calculated that he must have left London at five in the morning – and he seemed to have a vague purpose, as if he had gone shopping but forgotten his list.

Iona appeared from the house. 'Good Lord, Kit,' she said. 'Honestly: you are reckless with money. Are you all right?' She looked him up and down. Then she turned to the cab. 'Don't stay in there, for heaven's sake,' she called to the driver. 'Come and have some breakfast.'

'Well, I wouldn't say no,' replied the cab driver, folding up his newspaper and stashing it on the dashboard.

He and Iona went on ahead, into the house.

'Very reasonable,' nodded Kit, watching them go. 'You'd be surprised.' He was wavering on his feet a little. 'I've been dreaming about a cup of coffee since about Reading.'

Bones must have heard his voice from the field. She arrived in a skid of gravel and flung herself at his legs in delight, wriggling around his knees like a rope, over and over again. Then she suffered a fit of mad energy and coursed the gravel, turning circles and sending the stones flying before planting herself in front of him in a series of deep bows. 'Silly dog, and at your age you'll give yourself a heart attack,' said Kit, attempting to hide how pleased he was. He laid a hand on her head.

'She adores you,' said Alice in surprise. 'I had no idea.'

Inside, Kit drank coffee and refused all food. The taxi driver ate bacon and eggs and then retired for a doze. 'Just give me ten minutes' notice, mate,' he said to Kit, 'before you want to head off.'

Alice and Iona exchanged glances, wondering if there was a reason Kit had come and when – or whether – he would give it.

Iona said, 'It's a lovely day – it seems mad to be indoors. I've got classes in a minute, but why don't you two go for a walk or something?'

'A walk,' Kit repeated, as if he had never heard those words before. 'I don't feel like... that. But I'd like to be outside. I'm a bit cold, that's all.'

In private, Iona said to Alice, 'I'm not sure Kit's very well – he's awfully pale.'

Alice made a Thermos of coffee and took Kit over to the caravan. Swaddled in blankets, he lay on the grass with Bones. Alice sat back down on the step, not feeling as certain of herself as she had an hour before.

Kit pulled from his pocket a miniature bottle of brandy, the dregs of which he emptied into his coffee cup. Then he smoked the last of his cigarettes, drawing them one by one from his shirt pocket. 'Damn,' he said, agitated, 'I kept meaning to stop on the way and get more, but I forgot.'

'I expect there are some lying around,' soothed Alice.

'Or we can always go to Boscastle and buy some.' She was struggling to take the temperature of this encounter; she was surprised by wanting to accommodate him. Kit seemed so unlike himself that she was unnerved. He was soft and relaxed, one moment cuddling the dog, the next flinging his limbs out of the blankets and lying in a star-shape on his back.

Now he sat up, cross-legged, and covered himself up again. 'Brr,' he said. 'It's nice to be out of that taxi.'

'Do you have to go back to London today?' asked Alice. 'Your mum was chuffed to bits that you came.'

'Was she?' asked Kit. He examined Bones's ears, and then said, 'It's funny about Mum: I have this completely different person in my head from the one I find when I actually see her.'

'Which is better?'

'Oh, the real one, by a mile.'

'Well, that's the right way round.'

'Hm, yes.'

He inhaled smoke and tipped his head back to blow it at the sky. 'It's because I hated her so much, for pushing off, all those years ago.'

Alice was so startled she nearly fell off the step. 'You must both have been miserable,' she said, her voice careful, not wanting to frighten him into silence.

Kit said nothing for a moment, and Alice thought perhaps he would stop there. They both heard seagulls, crying overhead.

Then Kit said, 'Yes, we were. But of course, I didn't think about how she felt, because I was a teenager. And probably a bit of a bastard. I wanted her to be miserable. I thought she deserved it. I thought, *If she's going to push off and leave us, then sod her'.'*

'Why didn't you go with her?'

Kit considered, lying down again. Smoke escaped from his mouth and nostrils and blew away on the wind. 'I was punishing her, I suppose,' he said. 'I didn't know about Rosie, then. I didn't know why Mum was going, and she didn't say. It was years before I found out about Rosie.'

'But you must have known how unhappy your mum was?'

'Yes, but... I didn't think about it like that; I only thought about me. As far as I was concerned, she could have had two fresh black eyes every morning and I still would have expected her to stay put, for my sake. Are all teenagers that selfish?' He put one hand behind his head and went on, 'Also, there was Dad: you know what he's like. I was more frightened of making him angry than I was of making my mother unhappy – or myself happy, for that matter. If I'd gone with Mum he would never have forgiven me.'

The poignancy of this struck Alice to the quick. She felt full of compassion, as if she had not known anything about Kit until that moment. She searched for the word in her mind, and it came to her: intimate.

She had thought intimacy was something that stayed between two people once it had come – but then, she had thought that about happiness. It turned out that both were as fleeting as the shadows of the wind-blown clouds she could see flashing across the grass.

Feeling that she was putting out a hand towards him, Alice said, 'You don't have to stay there now.'

'What do you mean?'

'Only that… you're still living in the house. You never left.'

Kit was silent. Alice guessed that perhaps her sympathy had been mistaken for criticism. 'I'm not getting at you –' she began.

'No,' said Kit, sitting up. 'You're just calling me a big baby who never grew up.'

'No, I'm not,' said Alice, resisting the urge to giggle. In as conciliatory manner as she could, she said, 'All I'm saying is, the more I hear, the more everything makes sense… I wish I'd known –'

'You mean, I'm coming up with some good excuses for my rotten behaviour?' He rubbed his face up and down with both hands. 'What about your behaviour? But of course, I forgot, it's my fault, what happened, isn't it? Come on, here we are: let's cut the crap.'

'No,' said Alice, stunned. She tried to stop him – she did not want this in her face, not here. This was not allowed.

But Kit would not be stopped. 'What the fuck am I doing here?' he snapped, looking around and rising to his feet, angry, flinging off the blankets one by one. Bones scrambled to her feet, confused, afraid of his tone of voice. 'I was about to get laid! And now I'm getting a whole load of shit from you!'

'What?' Alice was fearful. Kit had become twice her size. His voice filled her ears.

'This is why I never take drugs, or do anything on the spur of the moment,' continued Kit, more to himself than Alice, patting his pockets. 'Because it *never fucking works*. I should have stayed where I was and shagged that gorgeous girl.'

'I have no idea what you're talking about.' Alice was shaken. She too got to her feet.

'No, why would you, because you're in la-la land, here in your tinky-boo fantasy life, where you bake scones...'

'*What?*'

'Oh, come on!' He had found a pair of sunglasses in his jacket, and now he put them on. Bones barked at him, once. 'This isn't real life!' he continued. 'This is a fantasy. This?' he cried, knocking on the caravan wall, 'This is just a doll's house!'

'Don't be such a bully!' sweated Alice. 'This is what I'm doing! I'm here; I'm happy.'

'Great,' said Kit, 'that's sweet. But please don't delude yourself that you're taking part in anything resembling reality. You're like one of those mental patients, making corn dollies in hospital between doses –'

Alice's mouth fell open. 'Oh my *God*,' she gasped, 'Don't –'

' – Eventually, you're going to have to come back to life.'

'Shut up!' yelled Alice in his face. 'Shut up! You know nothing! I'm *better* – ' She stopped, and then after a pause she went on, quite calm now, 'Is this your way of trying to persuade me to come back? To you? Because if so, I'd say it's not going very well.'

'No,' said Kit, subsiding, 'I came...' he tailed off. 'I don't know why I came.' He put a hand on top of his head as if he'd lost a set of keys.

Alice did not dare say, 'Did you come to take Bones?' in case he said, 'Yes'. She was quiet.

They stood in silence for a moment. 'I'm going to wake up that nice man,' said Kit with finality, 'and say goodbye to Mum.'

Alice stayed where she was, stupefied. She did not know what to do. She thought perhaps Kit would come and say goodbye, but then after a few minutes she heard the cab's engine start.

To her horror, Bones pricked her ears, gave a questioning *wuff* and set off for the gravel at a canter. Alice shouted, 'Bones!' and pelted after her. As they reached the front of the house, the taxi was pulling away and Bones accelerated after it. 'Bones!' called Alice, frantic, 'No!' The dog stopped, not knowing what to do, and glanced over her shoulder at Alice.

Alice could see Kit's head in the back of the taxi, but he did not turn round and the taxi drove on. Bones stood where she was, confused, watching it go.

Alice caught up with her and knelt down beside her, clutching on to her collar. Somehow – somewhere along the way – Alice seemed to have started crying. She clung to the dog for some minutes, holding her tight and sobbing into her collar.

Iona came out and found her there. 'We had a row,' Alice said.

'Oh dear,' said Iona, her hands on her hips. 'I hoped you might work something out! Perhaps not.' She looked at her watch. 'Shall we have a glass of wine and some lunch? All this drama! I think we deserve it.'

After food and wine they felt better. Iona rummaged in a chest of drawers in the sitting room and produced a box of photographs. Alice slid on to the kitchen bench next to her and they looked through them together.

'Dear me, don't I look young!' said Iona. 'Like a child.'

'Well, you practically were. What were you? Twenty? Younger than me.'

'Yes, that's right,' said Iona. She looked down at the photograph in her hands. 'Tod took this. He took all the photographs – I wasn't supposed to go near the camera. Look, it's Venice; we were there for the Biennale. I was so excited – I had hardly been out of Scotland, before I met Tod. He was very embarrassed to be with someone so unsophisticated – he kept speaking to everyone in Italian, to make up for it. He'd been in Italy during the war and he was pretty fluent.'

She stood up and went to the sink, picking up a tea towel and drying a bundle of cutlery, piece by piece. 'We were staying in such a smart hotel,' she continued, 'and I remember Tod was out on the balcony smoking, drinking whisky, I expect, and I was getting ready to go to a party, and little Kit, just a baby, was sleeping on the bed... I was wearing something Tod had bought me, and some wonderful shoes, and I was filled with – oh, I don't know,' she sighed and put a hand up to her mouth, considering. 'Happiness, I suppose. I could see him, outside, leaning on the balustrade, with the smoke hanging in the air... I felt very... *loving*, you know, one of those moments? Tender.' She laughed and shook her head. 'Anyway, I went outside and put my hand out, I was going to touch his shoulder, but he turned round first and he said, in this awful voice, "Those fucking shoes! I can't *stand* that noise for another second: clack-clack-clack! Round and round the room! Why can't you put them on at the last minute? That's what anyone with an ounce of sensitivity would do. Are you deliberately trying to make my life a misery?" On and on, like that. Like a dog on the end of a chain.'

She laughed again. 'I was so shocked! I started crying, I couldn't help it. And then… oh, he shouted! I'd trapped him; I'd ruined his life; he wasn't the sort of person who should ever have been tied down; fucking this, fucking that, fucking shoes, fucking baby… then, of course, I'd ruined my make-up, so he was even more furious, and he went off to the party on his own. I cried and cried. The girl came, who was going to babysit for us – I'd forgotten to ring down and cancel her – and she sat next to me on the bed and patted my shoulder. She didn't speak any English.' Iona took a deep breath, collecting herself. 'What was so awful, for me, was the gap between what I had been thinking, and what he had been thinking… I'd been walking around the room thinking how much I loved him, and he was sitting on that balcony hating me. Just *hating* me.'

There was a pause, then Alice said, 'But why did Tod marry you, if that's how he felt?'

'Yes, it's odd, isn't it? But you know, for all his modern art, he's very old-fashioned, Tod. Don't forget, he was born between the wars. His mother wanted him to marry me, and he adored his mother – she spoiled him rotten. Would have done anything for him, and vice versa. And *my* parents put a lot of pressure on *him* – my father wanted to get his gun out.'

'Was it all like that? I mean the marriage?'

'Yes: silence, or shouting. It was worse when Kit got older, because he had this little frozen face, waiting to find out which it would be. And if it wasn't me and Tod shouting at each other, it was Tod shouting at Kit: noisy toys, coloured pencils lying about… He threw a fit once when Kit put all his farm animals out on the sitting-room floor, and some art person came round, and there they were…' She started giggling. 'All these cows and pigs… You know, not white. Tod only liked white things.'

Alice started laughing too, but then Iona said, 'Tod kicked them all into the fire. With Kit standing there, watching.' They both stopped laughing and looked down at the photograph. 'Poor little boy.' After a moment Iona added, as an afterthought, 'He must have felt very peculiar, when you told him you were pregnant.'

Alice looked at her. The remark reverberated, like a struck tuning fork.

In the middle of the night Alice lay awake; restless; her thoughts unquenchable. She worried at her mind until, like pushing a splinter from her palm, something lay exposed on its surface, something she had not seen before.

Perhaps Kit had not wanted to have a baby because he was afraid of how he might treat it. He might not have known it himself, but still it might be true. She had never asked him why he did not want to be a father, because neither of them had admitted that this was the case. From the moment she had told Kit she was pregnant, they had skeetered away from each other like two marbles dropped on a wooden floor: that was the moment at which they had begun their charade and it had only been interrupted by chance, when the car came off the mountain.

Alice flushed; got out of bed; went to the window. She remembered that morning in Florida, driving from the Chicken Shack back to the church to collect her parents in the knowledge that there was another person in the car with her: her baby; Kit's baby.

She had imagined she might be pregnant but she had not been prepared for the sensation that came with the certainty of it. When she had looked at the second test and it too had read positive, she had felt as if someone had struck a match inside her. A little fire was lighted and as it took hold it had warmed her from the inside out. In that moment – and in every moment until the night at the Dead Sea – she had felt accompanied. She had wanted to feel comforted, cushioned like that for ever.

That morning, while her parents were holding hands and singing hallelujahs, Alice had had all her questions answered by a funny little plastic wand. Her homesickness, her lovesickness, her stomach-churning nerves – all had been banished. Driving back to the church, she had jogged up and down in her seat, saying, 'I'm going to have a baby', out loud, and then gasping to hear the words.

She had felt a far more important person than the child who had dropped her parents off an hour before; she had felt like the Alice who had eaten the cake labelled 'Eat Me', as if she had outgrown herself and her elbows and knees would come bursting out of her clothes. 'I will not tell them yet,' she had said aloud. 'They mustn't know.' She had worried that her feelings would be visible.

She had wanted her own way – to have the baby – and she had believed she was justified in expecting it. Without being explicit, she had made her position one of moral right. Pregnant, she had been unassailable. What Kit thought, or felt, she had registered – like a sudden draught over a fire – but not taken into account. She had not thought, *I can persuade him*, but rather, *There's nothing he can do*.

And then: not pregnant, and strangers. As if they had never known each other at all.

She placed a palm on the cold glass of the window.

Under the moonlight she could see the glow of the caravan, in the corner of the field. She frowned. Kit had spoiled it. But… she knew he was right: it was a toy. This life she had pictured for herself was as much a dream as the life of a flower-seller that she had imagined that night in London, driving home from Emmy's.

Today, everything had been upset and upended. Even Kit not wanting to take Bones away had not given her the pure pleasure she had thought it might. 'She looks so well,' he had said, patting her. 'She seems so happy here.'

Alice felt disorientated; wakeful; confused. She got back into bed, turning on to her side so that she faced the window. Shades of black and grey shifted in and out of her field of vision as clouds and treetops were disturbed by the wind.

She heard a muffled *Yip-yip… yip* as Bones dreamed, paddling the tips of her paws on the bedcovers. Alice watched her, not knowing whether to wake her or not – it always worried Alice that she might be having a night-mare, and not a dream at all.

Part Five

1

Rob had been trying to reach Kit since the party but had got no replies to his emails or text messages and no answer when he had tried to telephone. Kit was notorious for not responding so it was not unusual, but still Rob was beginning to go from being annoyed to being worried. 'Please don't bring it up again,' said Naomi, pausing in what she was doing and putting her fingertips to her forehead. 'Please will you go round and knock on the door because I can't bear to have this conversation with you *one more time.*'

Roles were reversed in some aspects of their relationship, Rob thought as he scooted up to Notting Hill. Naomi was the problem-solver with the male mind; he was the fretter, the person who would worry for weeks at a time but take no affirmative action. But when it came to practical matters he was useful: he could fix things. He knew that counted for a lot of points, with his wife.

He could rewire electric lights, and unblock drains.

He had once mended the washing machine by taking out the motor, drying it in the oven and putting it back again, upside down. He had fitted his scooter with his own-designed immobiliser so that it could not be jump-started and nicked. When Naomi had girlfriends round she boasted of the things he could do. 'The rabbit hutch? Oh, Rob made it for Charlotte's birthday,' she might say.

'You're so *lucky*,' the friends would chorus. 'My husband is *useless*.'

Not that there was much of that at the moment. He and Naomi were in the middle of a row that felt terminal ,which was why her voice had that expressionless tone he hated when she told him to go and look for Kit.

'You're not listening to me!' she had said, earlier in the evening.

'I am listening to you; I don't agree with you. You want another baby; I don't.'

'Don't speak to me like I'm an imbecile,' Naomi raged, sitting on her haunches and throwing pairs of pants into the washing machine. Rob hated standing over her; it felt unfair, like a caricature of a domineering husband, so he had gone into the kitchen and switched on the kettle. 'And don't run away! I haven't finished!' Naomi called after him. Gritting his teeth, Rob had opened and slammed all the kitchen cupboard doors, looking for a mug. 'Why don't you get one out of the sink,' yelled Naomi from the other room, 'and fucking well wash it up.'

Kit did not answer the doorbell straight away, but after five minutes of knocking and shouting through the letterbox, Rob heard his tread on the wooden stairs. A minute later the door was opened. 'Rob,' said Kit, sounding dazed. 'What are you doing here? Is everything OK?'

Rob looked at him. 'Are you growing a beard?' he asked.

'No,' said Kit, stroking his chin with one hand, 'I just haven't shaved.' He turned away from the door and Rob followed him into the house. 'What time is it?' he asked, pulling on a pair of shoes over his bare feet. 'I was asleep.'

'It's drinks time,' said Rob. 'Come on. I'm in desperate need of a drink. My wife is driving me mad.' He looked around him. 'What happened here?'

'The party. I haven't tidied up.'

'I can see that.'

'Well, there didn't seem to be much point.' Kit was defensive. With his foot, he pushed an empty Stella Artois box to one side of the hall. 'I've got to be out on Friday.'

'Where are you going to go?'

'I haven't decided.'

'*This* Friday?' said Rob. 'Hm.'

'Is that soon?'

'Yes, pretty soon.'

'Oh.' Kit fingered a cigarette out of his shirt pocket. He examined it with close attention before poking it into his mouth and lighting it.

'You look terrible,' said Rob, 'and this place is a shit-hole. Come on, we're going out. I'll buy you dinner. When did you last eat?'

When he got home he told Naomi what he had found. She was not interested until he said, 'The goldfish were dead, in the bowl.'

Naomi absorbed this information. Then she said, with one of those flourishes that made him remember how right he had been to marry her, 'Well, he had better come here. Go and pick him up – we can't leave him there in that state.'

'What, now?'

'Yes, now.'

'Christ, Naomi, I'm exhausted – and,' he added, remembering with relief, 'I'm over the limit.'

'Didn't stop you riding your scooter home. All right, I'll go. Ring him and tell him I'm on my way. Actually, it's better if I go, he'll do as I say.'

Kit was no match for Naomi. Charlotte moved into Billy's room and Kit was installed in Charlotte's, from where he did not stir. He slept; rose to drink tea; slept again. One night when everyone was asleep, Naomi heard him run a bath, but in the morning there was still no sign of him.

'How come,' complained Charlotte one morning before school, 'Kit gets to lie in bed all the time?'

'He's not very well,' said Naomi. 'He's tired.'

'Has he been sick?' she asked, thinking with some anxiety of her bedroom.

'No, don't worry, it's not that sort of ill. He lost all his favourite things, that's all, and it's made him sad.'

'What did he lose?'

Naomi thought for a moment, then she said, 'His girl-friend, his house and his dog. All the things he loved.'

Charlotte bobbed up and down on her heels, on the kitchen chair, with her spoon in her hand. This signified deep reflection. 'He lost a *house*? That's impossible,' she said in the end.

'You can ask him about it when he gets up.'

'Ah, yes,' said Rob, shaking out the newspaper and peering over it. 'When will that be, do you think?'

'When he wants to,' said Naomi.

Rob and Charlotte exchanged looks.

'I saw that,' said Naomi. 'OK, you two, get moving. Come on, Billy, eat up.'

Billy eyed her from his highchair and thumped the plastic tray.

After Rob and Charlotte had set off for work and school, Naomi took a cup of coffee and Billy into Charlotte's room. She drew the curtains back, opened the window and put Billy on top of the shape in the bed.

'Are you awake?' she asked, putting the coffee on the bedside table and sitting down on the rug on the floor.

The shape moved, and groaned. Billy giggled.

'Whosis?' mumbled Kit from underneath the duvet.

'Careful, it's Billy,' replied Naomi. 'Now listen: I've got some stuff to do in the house, so I'm going to leave him with you for a bit.'

'What?' said Kit, his tousled head emerging from under the covers. 'No, no – not qualified.'

'I'm not asking you,' said Naomi, 'I'm telling you.'

She lay back on the rug and stared at the ceiling while Kit digested her instructions. Then she rolled on to her front and looked under the bed. 'Ugh! Everywhere I look: hair. I spend my entire life picking hair off carpets and sweaters. It's disgusting.'

'You could shave all our heads,' said Kit, sitting up, holding Billy round the middle and looking into his face. 'Will he cry if I do this?'

'He might.' She sat up and they both looked at Billy, who stared back at Kit. 'Imagine, you might have had one of your own, by now,' said Naomi, lying down again.

'I know,' said Kit. 'Weird, isn't it?' He joggled his legs so that Billy tipped around on the duvet as if he were afloat on a choppy sea. Billy looked affronted, and then laughed.

'Are you sad about it?'

'No,' admitted Kit. 'Not about that. I don't think I ever understood it, not properly. It's complicated. I felt weird about it when it was happening, and weird when it wasn't. I feel sad about me and Alice. D'you know, I don't think we had one single genuine conversation from the moment she told me she was pregnant? We faked it all.'

Holding Billy steady with one hand, he reached out the other for the coffee. Naomi and Billy exchanged nervous looks.

Kit sipped, and thought how delicious it was. It didn't seem to matter any more whether or not the beans had been shipped from Ethiopia. It had been made for him by Naomi, and that made it good. This realisation was like peeling off a final layer of clothing before diving into water. He almost shivered. He put down the mug, looked Billy square in the face and said, 'I screwed it all up.'

But Naomi was half under the bed, pulling out

Charlotte's secret detritus. 'Christ, that bloody child,' she said, emerging with a banana skin, black and stiff, between her fingers. She sat up again. 'What? I didn't hear that last bit.'

Kit smiled, 'Oh, it was nothing. Go off and do your stuff if you like – we'll be fine.'

'OK. If he starts squeaking, shout. I'll be upstairs.'

2

The next time Emmy came, Alice was ready to go to the beach. 'I think I could even swim,' she said, 'if I wore a wetsuit.'

Jory rummaged in one of the sheds and emerged with a wetsuit which he chucked into the car boot. 'D'you want one?' he asked Emmy.

'No, thank you. I rely on the warming properties of lard,' said Emmy, lifting up her T-shirt and squeezing her tummy.

Jory laughed.

In the car park they had to wait for the beach to appear: it did not exist until the tide had gone almost all the way out, and then half a mile of sand emerged like a white hand from a winter glove. A few hours later it would be gone again.

People who knew came and waited. There were other

cars here, filled with other families, everyone smiling at each other because they shared the same secret.

The surfers were already in the water – they didn't care about *beach* – but Jory was not surfing today. 'Why not?' asked Alice.

Jory shrugged. 'I don't feel like it,' he said. 'I want to swim with the girls.'

Alice was suspicious. She had noticed him and Emmy flirting.

Jory went to the kiosk for tobacco and bought a bag of doughnuts from the man who made them to order: 20p each; six for a pound. When Emmy tasted one she said, 'Christ almighty, that's insanely good. He could charge ten pounds, and everyone would pay.'

There were two each, still hot, too hot to eat. They laughed at each other's faces, trying to eat them when they should have waited, blowing and puffing out their cheeks. Alice felt the sugar melt on her tongue, the squeeze of dough between her teeth and then the scald of hot jam. Jory opened a Sprite and they each took a swig to cool their mouths.

When he said there would be enough sand they piled out of the car and carried bags of food, drink, towels and clothes down to the beach. They carried their shoes, walking on bare feet in a few inches of water as the sea retreated, wave by wave. Alice, more feeble than the others, kept saying, 'Why not here?' Jory made her keep going further, further away from the car park, the road and everyone else. In the end he stopped and turned his back to the sea, looking up at the rocks.

'This'll do,' he said.

They set their camp up high on the sloping black rocks that ranged in tiers above the sand.

Alice didn't want to swim right away – 'I'll think about it' – so she sat with their clothes and watched Emmy and Jory in the surf. Jory ran in and dived and Emmy walked forward with her breath held and her fingertips brushing the water until she was up to her waist and a wave came and she had to go under.

Alice put two towels on top of each other, and sat on them. She drew up her knees and looked down at her bare feet, wriggling her toes. Then she squinted back at the sea where Emmy and Jory were submerged but for their two smooth brown heads, like seals' heads, bobbing beyond the break of the waves. They were talking, she could tell. She wondered how she would feel if they got together. She felt possessive about them both: Emmy because she was her sister; Jory because he had carried her out of the field that day.

Alice saw Emmy lie back in the water and float, and Jory dived, and disappeared. He was so strong, it was like knowing where the fire extinguisher was: Alice felt that nothing could go too wrong with him close by. Perhaps that was why she felt frightened that Emmy might take him away.

Alice looked in all the bags they had carried with them and found the Thermos. She unscrewed the lid and poured tea into a cup. Then she screwed the lid back on. Holding the cup between both hands, she watched the waves and decided whether to swim. *You don't have to*, she thought. But the feeling afterwards... she knew, she could see from the other faces emerging from the water below her, those joyous swimmers – *Alive! Alive!* – that it would be worth getting cold for. Swimming in the sea was a transporting experience: you felt it.

Unless, of course, she thought as she blew on her tea, *it was the Dead Sea.* In that salty sea there had been no life at all. She remembered the lifeguard saying, "Don't splash". Swim without splashing? Impossible. You could only do it on a day when there was no wind and no weather, or if you did not swim freely at all.

Above this beach gulls dipped and curled. Children ran on the sand in all directions. Alice smiled and watched, hugging her legs, resting her chin on her knees.

A little boy in shorts stomped past on the sand below her. He was talking solemnly to himself. 'I'm going to get some rocks,' he was saying, 'and put them in my bucket…' He carried a yellow bucket in one hand and a plastic spade in the other; his skin was painted in stripes of white sun cream. He was followed at a discreet distance by his father, also in shorts, trying not to look as if he was keeping an eye on things. He and Alice exchanged the faintest of smiles.

Alice did not think about Bean any more; the spectre had vanished. 'Please, Alice,' Emmy had begged her, sitting next to the bed, 'he's gone. But you're not.'

Alice had realised, in one of those long nights she had spent awake in the hospital – such coughing and groaning all round her she wondered how anyone could sleep – that it had long ago stopped being about Bean. At first, it was true, she had felt the loss of him like a stab from a sharp blade. But sadness was too clean a feeling; her conscience dictated that she feel something a little more dirty: shame, failure, self-disgust. So she had conjured up a tyrant whose job it was to accompany her everywhere and make sure she did not try to avoid her punishment. This was the tyrant who had spoken up when she was hungry.

The smallest children ran in circles, like puppies do sometimes, just for the fun of it. Looking down, Alice brimmed with delight; it was too much for her to sit still with; she had to get up and *do*.

She stood up and, hiding between the rocks, got out of her clothes and into the wetsuit. She looked down at herself and giggled.

Emmy appeared. 'There you are,' she said. 'What are you laughing at? Come here, I'll zip you up.' She was soaking wet and uninhibited: dripping all over the place; untucking her swimsuit from her bottom; shaking water out of her ears.

'I'm coming,' said Alice, 'but you've got to look after me.'

'Of course I will,' said Emmy, holding out her hand.

Down on the sand Jory joined them and they jogged towards the water in a line. 'OK?' asked Emmy, as they reached the sea.

'Yes,' said Alice, sounding as decided as she could. She trotted into the waves, slowing to a walk when the water came up to her knees, and then ploughing on, churning through the surf, lifting one foot and then the other until she was in up to her thighs. Then a wave came crashing towards her and she had no choice but to dive under it.

She came up the other side and swam, ten strokes, straight forward, until the shock had worn off. Emmy appeared beside her. 'How was that?' she asked.

'Fine,' said Alice, when she could speak. But no, it was better than that: it was tremendous. 'It's perfect,' she said. 'It's heaven.'

'Keep going,' said Emmy, 'or you'll get cold. I'll stay right beside you.'

Jory swam a fast crawl ahead of them, turned and swam back, and then pushed along beside them doing breaststroke, which made Emmy and Alice laugh. 'It doesn't suit you,' Emmy called to him.

Together they swam the length of the beach and approached the cliffs which bracketed one end.

In the lee of these black rocks the water did not roll in waves as it did near the sand, but slapped and danced, deep and free, with traces of white spume criss-crossing its surface. Emmy and Jory lay on their backs and let the water lift and push them wherever it chose, but Alice hung from the surface like a clothes peg on a line, treading water, her breath coming in tense gasps.

Each rise and fall of the water took them closer to the cliff which loomed above, blackening the sky. Gulls turned in the air, tumbling off the rock face, skewing towards the water and then angling away again.

Every moment Alice's terror increased. 'Is it safe?' she trembled. Her voice seemed to come out flat, reduced to nothing by the cliff wall in front. As they drifted into the shadow of the rock, the water became as black and impenetrable as coal. Now they could hear the harsh, erratic slap of water striking the cliff.

'It's fine,' said Jory. He turned himself upright and bobbed beside her.

Alice stared at the face of the rock directly in front of her, but she was overwhelmed. The cliff was too mighty. She turned away from it, looked down into the water and experienced a terrifying shock of vertigo, as if she were hanging by a thread at the very edge of space. *This black rock*, she thought, her head spinning, *is the earth itself*. She thought of it plunging down into the water, down and down, hundreds, thousands of feet to the bottom of the sea. She was floundering at the lip of an abyss; she longed to cling to the vertical surface; anything to stop herself from spinning off into the depths. She felt panic leap within her ribcage, opened her mouth and swallowed a gasp of water that made her cough.

Emmy and Jory paddled beside her, as careless as otters in the water. 'D'you want to float?' asked Emmy. 'Here, turn on to your back.'

Almost in tears, Alice did as she was told. Emmy trod water beside her and placed a hand lightly underneath her back, in a gesture of support. 'There,' she said. 'You see?'

'Don't go away,' Alice pleaded. 'Don't take your hand away.'

'It's all right, don't worry. Stretch out your arms.'

Slowly Alice laid back her head in the water, uncurling her body as if she were opening her fist, until she lay flat.

Her ears were filled with the spit and crackle of the

seabed. She stared straight up at a view split into two halves: blue and black; sky and cliff. She had the strangest sensation: *But why am I afraid?* she thought, *I am the water; I am the rock; I am the sky.*

Emmy said, 'I'm going to take my hand away.' And then she did.

Back on the rocks they dressed again and wrapped themselves in blankets, then sat cross-legged and ate roast chicken sandwiches and soup. 'Who made this?' Emmy asked, tasting it.

'Me,' said Alice. 'Well, me and Marcella Hazan. What do you think?'

'Not bad. Iona's got you cooking now, has she?'

'Only for me and her. In the evenings. I like it.'

'Maybe you should come and work for me again, but this time, in the kitchen.'

'Maybe I will,' said Alice.

'It might be weird,' said Emmy. 'See how you feel about it. Fuck!' she said then. 'It's cold, now.' She tucked her feet under the edge of Jory's blanket.

Alice saw the gesture, and looked down at her soup.

When they got home there was no sign of Bones. Alice stood in the field and called her over and over, but it was dark and she was too exhausted to go looking. The swim had swept every dreg of energy from her body and she felt like a wrung-out cloth. In any case, sometimes Bones did stay out late alone in pursuit of foxes and badgers.

Alice left Jory and Emmy on the sofa together

drinking wine and smoking Iona's pot. Alice felt shy of them; she said goodnight and they called, 'G'night!' in unison, and laughed. Alice climbed the stairs to bed, trying not to feel annoyed. After all, she told herself as she brushed her teeth, she did not want Jory for herself, and she wanted Emmy to be happy. So what was it? As she climbed into bed alone – no Bones tonight – she remembered with a pang those tranquil, blessed nights when she had loved Kit.

3

When Kit appeared at breakfast the whole family looked up and stared at him. 'Everyone has to be dressed for breakfast,' said Charlotte. 'Even Billy.'

'Oh,' paused Kit, whose hand was halfway to a croissant.

'You heard the lady,' said Rob from behind the sports pages.

'Oh good,' said Naomi, 'You're up. You can come to Granny's birthday picnic with us we're leaving at ten. And that goes for all of you, did you hear me? Ten o'clock.'

'Dear God,' said Kit, 'this place is...'

'And no swearing, thank you,' added Naomi before Kit went out of earshot. Rob lowered his newspaper and looked at his wife, feeling a deep and abiding love. He willed her to smile at him; they had not spoken in days.

'No,' she said, feeling his look but not returning it,

and continuing to feed Billy, 'I am still not speaking to you.'

Charlotte looked from one to the other and took another croissant off the plate.

In the car, Kit sat in the back between Charlotte and Billy so that he could stretch his legs out past the gearstick. 'You might get covered in food,' Charlotte said in a speculative manner, looking at Kit. Billy was waving a rice cracker from his seat.

'I don't mind,' said Kit.

Charlotte turned to the window and looked out. She had still to be impressed by Kit. After all, he had taken her room; he had spent the week in bed (and yet he was not ill: incomprehensible behaviour, as far as she was concerned), and she had been told that he had lost all the things he loved. Losing precious things was something Charlotte could understand but not admire. When she lost something precious of her own, she was furious with herself.

Kit did not seem to do anything useful. Before, when he had used to come round, he had smoked, and sometimes Rob, and even Naomi, had smoked too – Charlotte had sneaked down the stairs and watched them. This morning Kit had smoked on the front step she had seen him. At least it was outside, but it made her think he might be staying, which would not be good.

She remembered his girlfriend, Alice, the one she kept mentioning. One hot day when the four of them had been having a picnic in the park, Kit had appeared with Alice and his dog Bones. Alice was beautiful and had lovely long brown hair.

Another time, Kit and Alice had come for dinner and Naomi and Rob had discussed them at breakfast the next morning: 'She's practically still at school,' Naomi had said.

'No, she's not,' Charlotte interrupted, 'She's finished school *and* university. She has a job; she told me.'

'And when did you have this conversation?' asked Naomi. 'I thought you were in bed by the time they arrived.'

'She came in by accident,' said Charlotte. 'She thought I was the bathroom, and then she came and said hello and goodnight. I liked her. She said that when she was little she slept with the light on because of spiders.'

Kit encouraged Rob to drink wine and beer, which Charlotte disapproved of. It made him smell, and it made him stupid in the morning when he walked her to school. 'I'm never going to drink wine or beer,' she had said to him once when he had been particularly affected.

'Me neither,' Rob had said, sounding feeble.

'Great!' said Charlotte, thinking, *That was easy*.

But he had, that very same evening – she had seen the wine bottle on the table. 'I thought you weren't going to drink that any more,' she had said to him.

'It doesn't count,' he had replied. 'It's called "Hair of the Dog."'

'But you said.'

'Did you, Rob?' Naomi asked.

'I was joking.'

Charlotte was disgusted with him. 'Jokes are true,' she retorted, and went to have her bath.

So she associated Kit with these lapses in behaviour.

And here he was – sleeping in her bed, smoking on the step, sitting in the car and coming to Granny's birthday. If these things – lost girlfriend, lost house and lost dog – had been as precious to him as they should have been, he would have been out there looking for them, thought Charlotte, not enjoying himself and spoiling their day.

Granny was Naomi's mother. She lived in a cottage in Sussex, near Lewes, and every year on her birthday she held a picnic in her garden for her children and grandchildren. If it rained, the picnic was indoors, which was sometimes more fun, with games of Sardines. Today it was hot.

At lunch, along with the four of them, plus Kit, there would be Granny, and then Gramps (who hardly said anything) and their dog Beetle. Des, Naomi's younger brother, would come with Charlotte's cousins: two boys named Felix and Sam and a girl named Louisa, nicknamed Squeeze. Squeeze was the best thing about the whole day. She was one year older than Charlotte, and she and Charlotte would have been best friends if they had not been cousins already.

Last year the boys had sat in the sun all day in deckchairs and got very burned, which was bad because Des and their mother were getting divorced, and when she saw the sunburn she would be angry with Des. This was what Squeeze had told Charlotte, while Des was telling Felix and Sam off. Squeeze's mother was nice, but a bit scary. She had always stood watching them when they played Grandmother's Footsteps before the cake, and never joined in. Now she didn't come any more. Charlotte asked Squeeze if it was horrible, the divorce, and Squeeze made a face and said, 'It was more horrible before. What about your parents?'

'I was a baby,' said Charlotte. 'I only remember Rob.'

Finally came Ally, Naomi's youngest brother, who was 'hopeless' – at least that was what everyone said – and sometimes turned up, but not always. When he did, he sat on the grass and held Granny's hand while she sat in her chair.

Like Christmas, it was a day steeped in ritual (and, like Christmas, always teetering on the brink of argument). It was Naomi's job to bring pudding, so in the boot of their car were Rice Crispie cakes (made by Charlotte) and a Victoria sponge (made by Naomi) for tea, and a *tarte aux pommes* (made by Patisserie Valerie and bought by Rob on the way home from work) for lunch. There was also half a case of rosé, packed into two cool bags filled with ice.

Kit had seen the rosé going into the car and now he was thinking it would be just the ticket for when he arrived. This was going to be hell. His own family was bad enough – and that was only two people. other people's families? Siblings? Children? Intolerable. As far as Kit was concerned, the best thing about adult life was not being bossed around by others, but he did not want to go and stay in a hotel, and that meant doing what Naomi told him.

When they arrived he carried the wine in and then, trying to look as if he was being helpful, opened a bottle and poured himself a glass. 'Number one's all right, then?' said Naomi as she passed him, carrying the cake.

'D'you want a glass?' asked Kit.

'No, I'll wait,' she said.

Kit saw Charlotte eyeing him from the doorway into the garden, but when he looked at her, she turned away and ran outside. He felt the chill of her disapproval and resented it. *So she doesn't like me,* he thought. *What does it matter?* He took another swig of rosé.

Everyone seemed to have a job to do, even Des's two boys (both wearing black hooded sweaters despite the heat) who were carrying chairs out of the kitchen and into the garden. Kit went and stood outside where no one could see him doing nothing. The two girls – Charlotte and Squeeze – were running about on the lawn, picking up handfuls of mown grass and throwing them at each other, but gently, with giggles. Kit could not help smiling as he watched. Billy sat on the grass and occasionally Charlotte would swoop past him and sprinkle grass cuttings on his head, which made him laugh.

Kit went and sat on the grass with Billy, but the next time Charlotte swooped, she saw him and faltered.

'Can't I join in?' asked Kit.

Charlotte didn't answer, saying instead, 'Why aren't you in the house?'

'Everyone's busy helping.'

'You could help.'

'They're fine. It's nicer out here.'

'But you can't play with us, you're too big.' Charlotte's voice wobbled.

'OK, OK,' said Kit, holding up a hand and getting back to his feet. 'I'll go back inside. I was joking, anyway.'

He felt humiliated as he walked back across the lawn

towards the house. He turned once to see Charlotte was watching him, and saying something to Squeeze. Billy had started to cry now that the game had stopped.

Kit stepped into the cool and dark of the hall and, hearing a television, walked into a dark study where the shutters were half shut.

Sitting in an armchair, feet up on a stool, slept an elderly man. The television was showing a golf tournament. Kit slid a pile of newspapers across the sofa to make himself some room and sat down. Perfect. He could watch golf until someone came to tell the old man that lunch was ready.

But his satisfaction was short-lived. It didn't feel as clever as he had thought it would, sitting watching television in the half-dark, avoiding chores and hearing laughter from the garden. He felt his mood deteriorate, and he began to fidget. The golf was not sufficiently distracting.

He heard Rob's voice, 'In the study? Thanks, Charlotte.' The door flew open. 'What are you doing sitting here in the dark, Kit? You are odd.' The other man woke with a start, and more newspapers slid from his lap to the floor. 'Hello, John,' said Rob to him.

'What? Rob? Is that you? What time is it?'

'About one. We're all here: lunch in ten minutes. Kit, can you come and get involved?'

Naomi's mother sat at a table under a tree. Kit refilled her glass and wished her a happy birthday. 'Oh you are kind. And thank you for coming to my party! I'm sure there are things you'd rather be doing, on a Saturday.'

'Don't be silly,' Kit lied.

Naomi brought over a plate of food. 'Here you are, Mum,' she said. 'Any news from Ally?'

'Tied up at work, he said. He left a nice message.'

'Hm,' said Naomi. 'Kit, aren't you eating? Why don't you go and help yourself.'

They all sat at a table under a tree to eat and then lay down on the grass to complain about how much they had eaten. Rob and Billy fell asleep; John went back indoors to the golf; Naomi murmured to her mother at the end of the table. Kit tried to talk to the boys, but they edged away from him.

'We've got to clear the plates,' said Sam. Or was it Felix? They both got up and started stacking.

When they had gone Des rolled over and said, 'God, what did you say to them? They never help clear up. They must have been desperate.'

'De-es,' remonstrated Naomi.

'What? I'm just saying.'

Kit felt embarrassed again, and when Naomi said, 'You have to be nice to Kit, Des. He's a bit fragile', he did not feel better. *Life amongst people is hard*, he thought. It was easier to spend the day alone.

He was almost asleep, lying with the tin of Rice Krispie cakes on his stomach, when a shadow fell across him.

'You can't eat all of them,' said Charlotte, staring down at him. 'They're for the little children.'

'But they're so good,' said Kit, aiming to please, 'I can't stop.'

Charlotte frowned and stood on one leg. 'It's rude to eat them all.'

Kit lifted his sunglasses, sat up and looked at her. He felt very tired. 'I haven't eaten them all. I've had three. Take them away if you want to.'

Charlotte bent down and took the tin away without another word.

'She doesn't like me,' said Kit, lowering his sunglasses and lying down again.

'Well,' replied Naomi, 'are you surprised? You're not exactly child-friendly. And she thinks you don't care about your dog, which in her opinion is your most heinous crime.'

'What happened to your dog?' asked Naomi's mother with some suspicion.

'Nothing happened to her,' said Kit, sounding fractious. 'She lives with my ex-girlfriend.'

On the way back to London everyone was tired. Billy woke up and started yelling. 'Too much sun,' said Naomi. 'Stop the car, Rob, and I'll swap places with Kit.'

Kit's head was thumping. He wanted to go home and doze in a darkened room. *Too much rosé,* he thought, *and too many bloody children.*

Rob pulled over in a layby and Naomi and Kit changed places. Billy, delighted to see his mother again, stopped crying at once.

'He probably woke up and thought, *Who's that horrible man sitting next to me?*,' said Charlotte in a considered way. 'I know I would, if I was him.'

Rob turned his snort of laughter into a cough. Naomi did not respond to Charlotte straight away but she thought for a moment or two and then said, 'Tomorrow, Charlotte, Kit is going to take you to orchestra.'

Charlotte sat up as if she had been electrocuted, and gripped the headrest of the front seat in both hands. 'Ow,' Rob remonstrated, 'mind my head.'

'But,' said Charlotte, 'it's the concert.'

'I know, pet. But Rob has to take Marvin to the vet, and Billy and I have a tea party.'

'But...' Charlotte opened and shut her mouth, 'you have to come.'

'Sorry, darling, not this time.'

'I don't want to do it, then.'

'Charlotte,' Naomi's voice took on a faraway tone and she scratched a midge bite on her elbow as she said, 'we're not having a discussion. I'm telling you what will happen tomorrow: you'll play in the concert and Kit will go with you.'

Charlotte made a muffled squeaking noise and gripped and ungripped the headrest with her hands.

Kit had no wish to spend time alone with Charlotte but was nonetheless affronted by her reaction. 'Come on, Charlotte,' he said, embarrassed to hear the desperation in his own voice, 'we might have fun.'

Charlotte did not look at him. 'Oh please, Mum...'

'That's enough. Stop being silly – you're hurting Kit's feelings.'

Charlotte subsided into her seat.

Rob allowed himself a smile and glanced at his wife in the rear-view mirror. Their eyes met and they exchanged a confidential look. Rob decided to follow up the advantage and made a 'kiss' face at her. Naomi rolled her eyes but continued to smile. She was still smiling as she kissed

Billy's forehead and looked out of the window. Rob let out a long breath: at last, he was out of Coventry.

4

Kit was woken by his telephone. It was dark, and the inside of his head felt sticky from all the rosé he had drunk the previous afternoon. He grabbed the telephone and answered the call without looking to see who it was, fearful of its waking someone else in the house. He clutched a pillow under his other ear. 'Whosis?' he mumbled, yawning, 'Wha' time is it?'

It was Alice. Her voice was clear but trembling, like a bicycle bell on a cobbled street. 'Kit,' she said, 'I'm sorry to call in the middle of the night. But I thought...' she tailed off.

'Alice,' Kit said. He sat up, one hand on his head, and tried not to think about cigarettes. 'Are you all right?'

The trembling voice began again. 'Ye-es,' it said, 'I'm fine, it's just – it's about Bones.'

'Bones?' he repeated. The picture that had formed in his mind, of his mother lying in a hospital bed with tubes sticking out of her nose, was wiped as suddenly as if he had changed the channel. It was no good; he was going to have to smoke. 'Listen,' he said, 'can I call you straight back?'

There was a pause. 'All right. But will you?'

'Of course I will. I've just got to get up and have a pee, and find my fags.'

'Is this a bad time? Is there... someone there?'

'Here? What, in bed?' He gave a short laugh. 'Come off it. No, I'm at Rob's. Stay by the phone; I'll call you in two minutes.'

He hung up, got out of bed and picked his jacket up off the floor, feeling for cigarettes and finding them in the top pocket. He put the jacket on over his T-shirt and pyjama bottoms. 'In this house,' Naomi had told him in her 'Captain of Games' voice, when he had first arrived to stay, 'you will wear pyjamas. I don't want an incident, with you frightening Charlotte in the night.'

'God forbid,' Kit had responded nervously.

In the kitchen he drank a pint of tap water and then refilled the glass with Ribena and carried it out of the front door and on to the step, along with the cigarettes and a packet of Swan Vestas from the mantelpiece.

Outside was the velvet plush of a summer's day before dawn, neither dark nor light, the street as quiet as a church. Kit propped the front door open with a copy of the *Yellow Pages* from under the hall table, had a discreet pee between the bins and the hedge, and then sat down on the step, lighting a cigarette and pressing 'recall' on his telephone.

There was no signal at Trebartha so he could picture Alice exactly, waiting beside the only plugged-in telephone in the house. 'Is that you?' she asked, answering on the first ring.

'Yes, it's me,' he said. 'Sorry about that.'

'No, *I'm* sorry, to wake you and everything,' she said in a rush, 'It's just that I thought I'd better call – I kept thinking I wouldn't need to, but now – '

'What's happened?' he asked, exhaling smoke. 'Has she been run over?'

'No, no – I mean, I don't know.' She paused and then quickly said, 'I've lost her, I can't find her –' and her shivering voice shattered into pieces. Now she was crying, but she struggled on: 'She disappeared; she's gone, and I don't know where... I can't find her, I've searched and searched...'

Kit suddenly found he was floundering too. It was not Bones who filled his mind; it was only Alice. He felt winded by sympathy; breathless with it. Her distress was so palpable that she almost took shape in front of him. He wanted to pull her towards him; he could hardly bear not to be able to.

'Are you there?' she asked.

'Yes, yes, of course I am,' he replied, but he had been overwhelmed; he could say nothing more.

'Oh, Kit,' Alice sobbed, mistaking his silence, 'I'm sorry...'

At last he gathered himself and said, 'No, stop it, Alice: it's not your fault. You didn't lose her; she just went.' He repeated, 'It's not your fault.' The cigarette burned between his fingers.

'But I've got to find her...'

'No, you don't,' he said with emphasis, standing up and gesturing at the sky with his free hand. 'You mustn't think that. You probably won't find her – she could be anywhere, but that's not the point... The point is, you can't go on thinking it's up to you...' He flicked his cigarette end into the road and lifted his head to stare up at the brightening sky. After a pause he continued, 'Look, Alice: if she's gone, she's gone. Please don't... You mustn't...' He took a deep breath. 'It was an accident. It just happened.'

There was a silence between them which seemed to go on and on, but it was a silence of consent. In its wake Kit heard the London birds begin to whistle their cautious chorus, bolder each moment. He felt the skin prickle under his shirt.

In the end Alice said, not crying now, 'If I find her...' She paused, then went on, 'If I find her, shall I bring her back?'

It was not the clattering voice of the hospital bed; it was the brimming voice that he recognised, and the grain of hope in it, that smallest trace of an appeal, went straight to his heart.

'Oh, Alice,' he said, his shoulders braced to take the weight of it, 'you don't have to find her, to come back...'

5

The next afternoon Charlotte put on her coat without a word and told Kit it was time to go.

'Have you got your music?' asked Naomi, 'and your clarinet?'

'Of course I have,' said Charlotte. She had not forgiven her mother.

'Come here and let me do your hair.' Charlotte stood in front of Naomi and allowed her hair to be smoothed into a ponytail. 'There.' She held Charlotte's shoulders for a moment and kissed her behind each ear. 'Perfect. Good luck – and don't forget: breathing.'

Charlotte tugged away, saying nothing. Kit, swallowing the dregs of his tea, watched her. 'Do I need to bring anything?' he asked. 'Ear plugs?' Naomi gave him a look and Charlotte stalked out of the room.

'That was not helpful,' said Naomi.

'Oh, come on – it was a joke.'

'You can be such an arse, Kit,' said Naomi, shaking

her head. 'Be nice, will you? And bring her back. I don't want you having a row, and her running off.'

'Christ! Don't say that,' said Kit in alarm.

'And Kit,' said Naomi, as he turned away, 'try to *participate* a bit, will you?'

'What? In the music?'

'No... just, generally.'

They walked in silence to the bus stop, but when they stood waiting Kit said, 'Let's have a nice time, shall we? I want to.'

Silence.

'OK, maybe not *nice*,' he joked, 'but it can still be all right.' He looked sideways at her, and saw that she had pulled her ponytail over her mouth to hide her smile. 'So,' he continued, 'where shall we sit on the bus? Upstairs? Downstairs? Front? Back?'

Another pause, and then, 'Upstairs at the front.'

When the bus came Charlotte had to show Kit how to use Rob's Oyster card. She was mortified. 'Haven't you been on a bus before?' she asked when they had sat down.

'Not for years,' said Kit. 'I take taxis.'

'You must be rich. Taxis are expensive, Mum says.'

'She's right. And, I am.'

Charlotte pondered this news, frowning out of the window. 'If you're so rich why don't you have your own house? And your own bedroom?'

'I lived in my dad's house, and he's sold it, so I've got to get another one.'

The bus stopped at a crossing on Shepherd's Bush

Green. They watched people pouring across the road in front of them. 'Ants,' said Kit. 'It's like an ant farm.'

'No, it's not,' frowned Charlotte. 'They're *people*. And anyway, ants don't live on farms, they live on hills.'

For some reason this struck Kit as funny and he laughed. Charlotte turned and looked at him. 'But they *do*,' she said.

'I know; they do; you're right.'

The room into which Charlotte led Kit, which was known by pupils and teachers as 'Assembly', smelled exactly as his school had, and perhaps every school in the nation did.

Charlotte took her instrument case away from Kit and handed him her sweater to look after. 'I don't mind if you want to go and do something else,' she said. 'You can come back when it's over.'

To hear her comment made Kit feel ashamed of himself. 'No,' he said, 'don't say that – I'm staying. I want to hear you play.'

On a raised dais at one end of the room children, most of them older than Charlotte, were unpacking their instruments and their sheet music. With a wordless look, which Kit interpreted as a mute appeal for him not to embarrass her, Charlotte slid away from him to join the others.

Parents, much more formally dressed than Kit, were seated close together on rows of plastic chairs. As Kit walked up the central aisle the women, who were speaking as intently to one another as if they were discussing secrets of state, lifted their heads and appraised him with cool stares. The fathers glanced up once and then back down again at the Sunday newspapers or Blackberries in their laps. Kit was self-conscious. He wrapped Charlotte's jumper round his neck like a scarf, for comfort. He took a seat at the edge of the room.

Charlotte's expression was serious as she adjusted the music on her stand. The clarinettist next to her was a red-haired boy of about thirteen, Kit guessed, who polished first his instrument and then his glasses with a large yellow duster. He and Charlotte did not speak to one another but exchanged a look and a half-smile of united purpose. All the children seemed to regard the event with grave responsibility but the parents kept up their continuous stage whisper punctuated by the occasional loud laugh, followed by a flurry of *shush-shush*.

The music teacher was a good-looking man in his thirties. In a calm, devoted manner he helped the children with their instruments and made sure their music stands were set at the right height. Without looking at the audience, he stepped on to a box that stood in the middle of the dais and raised both hands. Kit, from his position at the side, saw his face give a corresponding lift of encouragement. In one motion, the children raised their instruments. The next moment was quite still, and all the parents stopped talking. Then the music began.

Kit, from the moment he had seen Charlotte take her seat, had been fighting an unexpected surge of emotion, and now his reaction became yet more urgent and surprising: he thought he was going to cry, and he did not know if he could stop himself.

It was not that the standard of musicianship was high,

for it was not, and indeed, hardly a moment passed without someone's music drifting in sheets to the floor, or a metal stand toppling over with a crash, or an instrument letting out a noise like a captured animal. But the expressions on the faces laid out before him showed a seriousness, a concentration – a commitment – that he wished would show on his own face or that he could feel in his own life.

With desperate intent, he examined what lay in front of him – the puffed cheeks; the strands of hair escaping from the girls' clips; the boys' feet crossed under their chairs; the taut composure of one and all – and for a moment he stopped thinking about himself. He thought of Alice and her voice on the telephone, and here were his tears at last.

6

After speaking to Kit, Alice lay awake all night and listened to the scattering sound of rain blown against the window. It was a sound which she had used to love; now it had become nightmarish, a ceaseless torture. The wind blew in from the sea in drifting, damp gusts. She lay on her side and stared out at the grey blotting-paper dawn.

When it was light enough she got out of bed and pulled her jeans on underneath her nightie. Downstairs she made coffee, poured cereal into a bowl and ate it standing up, looking out of the kitchen window at the wet green field and the miles of dark woods which stretched away from her. They had seemed like paradise before, but now they seemed huddled and secretive, as if whispering some malevolent conspiracy. *Somewhere in there,* she thought to herself, *is Bones.* She knew the dog might be dead by now, as everyone else seemed to think she was, but Alice had to try to find her, *just one more day.* Bones might still be all right, she might be caught up in a bit of wire by the collar, and waiting to be set free.

She had spent the previous six days on an almost continuous search for the dog. The truth was, she did not know what else to do. On the first day she had thought at any moment Bones would do as she always did: walk back into the kitchen, take a long drink and then collapse on to the floor with a thud like a stack of books toppling over. As night fell Alice had stared out into the field until her eyes ached, imagining every flickering shadow was Bones creeping back up the hill alongside the hedge, sniffing at the tufts of fur left by rabbits on the sheep wire.

Alice had left the back door open and all that first night she had waited to hear the dog's long toes *click-click-clicking* up the stairs to her bedroom. But there was nothing; only the owls shrieking and the scrummage of the badger on the gravel, coming past the house on its evening promenade.

On the second day she had set out to find her, truly believing that she would. She had walked all day, calling and calling, in the woods. When her legs gave up she had to telephone Jory from a phone box on a lane, somewhere she had never been before. He had come to fetch her and they had driven in silence back to Trebartha. In the yard he switched the car's engine off, and she sat and cried until she had given herself a headache. Jory had said nothing, passing her his rollie every now and again and waiting until she had finished.

Out in the field in the dark that night she had called,

whistled, sobbed and finally begged: 'please come back', with the long, wet grass dragging at her jeans and her hair plastered to her head in the rain.

And every day since she had stumbled through the woods, pushed her way through shoulder-high bracken, crawled into thickets of blackthorn, scoured ditches, walked the length of barbed-wire fences, opened barn doors and called into their hollow, dark interiors, searched along the roadsides, for miles, looking. She could not stop looking, not yet, not knowing what had happened.

'It's not just the dog,' Iona had said to her, 'it's everything.'

'It may be everything,' said Alice, in a voice like dishes being stacked, 'but right now, it's the dog.'

Emmy, on the telephone, did not know what to say. 'It happens,' she said, and, 'She was an old dog.'

'But where is she?' Alice asked, piteous. 'I have to find her.'

'Maybe she was stolen,' suggested Emmy.

'But who would steal an old yellow lurcher?' asked Alice, and started crying again.

'You've got to tell Kit.'

'I can't, yet,' Alice said. 'I've got to find her. I lose everything of his.'

Jory gave her a dog whistle because her voice had all but given out, but it sounded even more like a plea than calling Bones's name. It was the long, roaming wail of a seabird. Alice could not bear to blow it.

And now the dog had been lost for a week, and she had told Kit, but still she set out again and walked through the woods, following deer paths and poking sticks into fox's earths, calling with her hoarse voice, 'Bones! Bonesy!' and trying to whistle, but her lips and mouth were dry, and nothing came out. Her feet trod, trod, trod and her mind swung like a pendulum: *Bones... Bones...* Every few minutes she stopped; held her breath; listened. Sometimes she thought she heard yelping, but when she turned her head to hear it again, there would be nothing.

She crossed the stream and climbed up the hill on the other side, curling up through the trees, unable to remember, now, whether she had come this way before or not. What did it matter? She had begun to think she would never find the dog, alive or dead.

She crept towards the top of the hill, her legs torn at by brambles and her boots slipping in the leaves under her feet. A movement caught her eye. Something was struggling, there in a fence, a bit of mesh, sheep wire, stuffed into a hole in an old wall, here in the middle of the woods where she had thought there were no fences.

Her heart leapt – *Bones!* – but it wasn't. She saw as she drew closer it was a deer, a fawn, the colour of milk chocolate, its eyes jumping from its head in terror and wire twisted in a loop around its foreleg, making a snare. It had tried to jump the fence and one foot had trailed and caught in the netting, tethering it. Alice had seen the remains of other deer who had died in this way, on other fences: a leg bone still hanging in a twist of wire; a skeleton on the ground below. Once they were caught they could never hope to free themselves.

There was a stamp from the patch of bracken beyond the fence and Alice saw a doe treading from hoof to hoof, watching Alice's approach with a wide, horrified gaze. The mother. She had not left her fawn, and could not bear to leave it now, despite Alice being so close. Alice stared at her. She seemed ready to spring away into the undergrowth; her ears flicked back and forth and her hooves moved in a constant, restless motion, as if she were treading water. The fawn started to struggle and make an awful mewling bleat, an uncomprehending cry.

Alice opened her mouth. Her own voice surprised her: 'It's all right,' she said, 'I'm going to get you out.'

She took off her jacket and crept towards the trapped creature, ignoring its mother who stamped and trembled, rushing away and then tiptoeing back in horror to watch what Alice was doing. 'Shush, shush,' said Alice, creeping closer, and as soon as she could reach it, wrapping her jacket around the fawn's struggling body. It felt like a bundle of twigs, under her arm. She tucked the packaged body against her own, holding it firm, keeping its covered head clamped in her armpit. When the fawn had gone still – *I surrender* – she examined the wire.

She saw she would have to make enough room in the wire noose to slide its hoof out. She started to worry at it, gradually to fit her fingertips between the thin strand of wire and the fawn's leg, forcing them to part, getting her fingers underneath and prising the metal away. Flies buzzed away in a hot, fizzing cloud as she separated wire from flesh, and she saw a thin trickle of blood begin to ooze out of the animal's leg and on to her fingers. As she worked away at the wire she spoke in a low, steady voice: 'If I do this for you,' she said, 'will you give me my dog back?' It felt as if every pair of eyes in the woods behind her was watching; everything held its breath; the trees stopped rustling and pattering with rain; the birds fell silent. She worked away at the wire, her fingers beginning to bleed and the fawn's leg, bleeding, bleeding, and its blood trickling down inside her sleeve to her elbow. 'Please,' she muttered, 'give Bones back to me.'

When she had made enough room she fitted the animal's hoof back through the loop. She looked at the cut. Would it bleed to death? She thought not – more likely it would die of shock. She lowered the animal, still bundled up in her coat, to the ground, and unwrapped it. It stood, staggered, fell, got up, fell again. It tested its leg – by a miracle, not broken. Its mother perched, trembling, on the brow of the hill a few yards away. The fawn shook itself from head to toe and trembled away at a three-legged canter, holding its leg up, then touching it to the ground, then hopping again. When it was near enough, the mother turned and wheeled into the bracken. They both disappeared.

Alice stayed where she was, kneeling on the ground, deep in the leaves that lay banked beside the fence. Flies clouded around her head. After a moment or two she put her jacket back on and examined her shaking hands. Blood.

It will probably die, she thought.

But she had done what she could: at least it would not die there, tied up in the fence, its anguished mother standing beside it.

Not knowing why – not pausing to wonder why – she followed the deer up to the brow of the hill along a path trodden, by their sharp hooves, deep into the soft, mealy soil. Where there were no trees there was wet, steaming bracken grown to shoulder height, and she had to push through using all her weight, as if she were walking through water. The wet soaked through her cotton jacket right to her skin in a second, but the smell of the bracken cleared her head. At the brow of the hill she came to a broken-down wall – long, ambling and moss-covered – which she climbed over, jumping down into a clearing.

It must at one time have been a small field. The wall, though fallen down in places, still suggested a square. In one corner there were foundations where a barn had stood, and stones were piled up in heaps. The clearing, overhung by huge ash trees at either end, was free of bracken and Alice could see by the flattened-down patches in the long grass that this was somewhere the deer came to sleep. There was no sign, now, of the fawn and its mother.

As she looked around her she saw, from the corner of her eye, two crows take off from the long grass and flap away, low to the ground. At the edge of the clearing they turned, folded their wings and hung in one of the ash trees, sitting still to watch her. They seemed reluctant to abandon the field altogether.

They were insolent in their manner, like children who, when told to stop playing with a bonfire, kick stones as they walk away. A question mark, like a match being struck, appeared in Alice's mind. She turned and walked through the long grass to the point where the crows had been perched. As she drew closer she saw that the wet grass lay flattened and streaked with slime and gore. A commotion seemed to have taken place there, and the question mark in her mind was replaced by a knock of certainty.

There was the carcass, stretched out on the ground. There was no mistaking it for anything else: it was a dog, it was her dog. Bones, or what had been her once, was lying on her side as if she were still running, as if she had been stopped dead in flight by a lightning strike. Her front paws were stretched away from her hind legs as if she were leaping for an imagined goal. Perhaps she had been.

On the grass around her body, parts of her were strewn about: gobbets of wet fur and strips of skin. Intestines, grey in colour, were looped out of the hollow cavity of her gut, spilling on to the grass. No doubt foxes had fought over her, before the crows. There was no skin or flesh left on the carcass, no lips, no fur. Her head was a peeling, grey, fleshless skull, the teeth bared in a grimace, the eye sockets drumming with rain water. Maggots tumbled out of her where her tail – now a wet, grey skewer – had been almost separated from her body. Rain splashed into a puddle of dark red blood, in the empty ribcage. There was no heart, no liver, nothing left inside at all but bone and putrid, inedible matter. She had been eviscerated.

Alice stood and stared, registering nothing except what she saw, as if someone had pressed the mute button. *This is what happens when you die*, she thought. *The crows come and eat your body*. It started to rain again, and water dripped off Alice's nose and into the dirty grey mess on the ground. *My friend*.

She rubbed the end of her nose with a finger, and bent to look at Bones's face, or what remained of it. As she leaned down towards it, the stench of decay reached up from the ground and grabbed her, all the way from her nostrils to her stomach, and she gagged. Suddenly there was no fresh air, no escaping the stink of rotting flesh that clouded the air like smoke. There was no getting away from it; she took an involuntary step back.

The dog was dead.

But she had found her.

She did not want to leave Bones out here like this, but nor could she carry her home; it was too far, and Bones was too heavy. And there was nothing – Alice frowned – nothing to carry. Not really.

But how would she dig a hole? With her hands? She walked over to the wall and paced alongside it, searching, getting torn at by brambles and stumbling into holes covered by dead leaves. The rain seemed to intensify and batter on the hood of her jacket with the insistence of a maniac.

She came to a part of the wall where the branch of a holly tree had grown between the stones, pushing a heap of rocks on to the ground. Here. She would scoop out a shallow hole and lie the dog next to the wall, and then cover her with these leaves and these big stones. If she made a pile high enough, no scavenger would be able to get at the remains.

Alice rubbed the rain off her nose again. The smell was still in her nostrils. She bent and pulled the heap of fallen rocks apart until she had cleared a shallow place, a bed, the right size for Bones. Blood thundered in her ears. She scooped out leaf mould until the loamy soil, the colour and texture of coffee, was revealed underneath.

When she stood up again it was very quiet. The rain

had lessened, still pattering on the leaves above her head, but not soaking her beneath. She imagined lying down in this warm little place, and going to sleep.

When she turned back to the clearing one of the crows had come back and was poised on Bones's body, angling its head in different directions. Alice shouted, 'Hey!' and ran towards it, waving her arms. The crow looked at her for a moment and then took off again, as unhurried as before. Alice said, 'Get off her!' and then the words stuck in her throat and she gasped, and sobbed, and caught her breath. She knelt for a few moments in the wet grass.

She was surprised by herself: she was not sad. She had been sad before, when Bones had been lost. She had felt as if she too had been eviscerated. But now, no, it was not the time to be sad, it was time to put the body in the ground. She had a physical task to perform, and a responsibility to do it right. She was... relieved.

She walked back to the dog and stood looking down, her brain clicking into activity like a wound-up clock. She wondered how she was going to get what lay there from the grass to the wall. She needed a stretcher. A body bag.

She emptied the pockets of her cotton jacket and then took it off and laid it flat on the ground, next to Bones's body, as if she were going to sit down next to her. Then she gritted her teeth and took hold of a front and a hind leg, intending to slide the body on to her jacket.

The entire hind leg came away from the body, with a clicking sound, into her hand, as if she were jointing a chicken. Alice stood still and looked at the leg in stupe-faction. She didn't know what to do with it now. She put it down on the jacket, turning her mind from what had happened, and tried again, holding the remaining back leg and both at the front. The stink was so overwhelming her eyes started to water. She turned her head away and dragged at the body.

This time the remains held together and she slid the carcass on to her jacket. Bloody rainwater poured out of Bones's insides on to the grass, and all over Alice's boots. She could feel a tender mash of wet skin and bone grinding under her hands. She had left a slimy trail of guts, blood and greasy clots of fur on the grass, but she had done it. She turned away, holding her hands as far away from her body as she could. She took gulps of fresh air. The smell seemed to have infused the very deepest recesses of her lungs. She could almost feel it inside her body.

When she turned back to her task she saw that the dog's tail had come away from its body and maggots were tumbling in fury around it, on the grass. Alice frowned. She bent to pick up the tail, and noticed her hand was steady as she laid it beside Bones, on the coat. She tried to tuck the body up together, to make it look as if the dog was curled up, sleeping, as she'd used to do, with her front and hind paws touching and her head bent to her chest. For a moment she gasped with sorrow – *Bones!* – then she lifted the jacket up around her and, holding the corners and the sleeves, dragged the whole sodden, rotten, gruesome package across the clearing to the wall.

There seemed to be blood leaking through the coat, making a great red stain, but it didn't matter, they were there now. Alice slid the parcel into the scooped-out place she had made in the ground, and knelt down to swaddle the body in the jacket.

Kneeling, she packed handfuls of dead leaves, then

small rocks, and then larger ones, around that sodden parcel. She began to speak. Quietly she said, 'You'll be safe here, don't worry. It's all right.' As she spoke, and as she worked with her hands, the tears began to pour out of her. *Bones! Bones!* But she carried on packing stones together, one over the other, until she had put the largest one she could carry on top and she knew that the grave would be safe.

When it was done she stood up and the blood sang in her ears. She nearly blacked out. Then, everything that was not Bones came flooding back into her head in a torrent.

She was drenched; she was tired; she was miles from home. She had buried her jacket, and was now dressed in a shirt and jeans, both of which were soaked through. There was rain in her boots, from kneeling in the wet grass. She had to get going – she needed food, clothes, warmth – before she made herself ill again.

She looked down at the place for a last time, then, wrapping her arms around herself for comfort, she started back through the woods towards home.

7

Charlotte was elated after the concert and forgot to be disapproving of Kit, chattering to him non-stop as they made their way home. Waiting to cross the road, her hand stole into his – Kit felt his heart expand – and so with a new confidence Kit suggested they walk across the park. They continued to walk hand in hand and Charlotte pulled on Kit's arm if she sensed his concentration drifting.

Beside the Albert Hall they sat down on a bench to wait for the bus. Kit said, 'Perhaps you'll play your clarinet in there one day.'

Charlotte squinted over her shoulder at the round red walls of the concert hall. 'Yes, perhaps,' she said in her poised way.

'That's where I met Alice.'

'Really?' Charlotte was surprised. 'How?'

'Well, there was a big party, a charity thing, in the summer. It was a dinner, very smart, and an auction to raise money for something – Russian orphans, probably. Anyway, they were selling things, you know, holidays and cars and things, and they sold me.'

'How do you mean?'

'You know I paint pictures of people?'

'Yes.'

'So, someone pays money, and I paint their picture, but instead of me getting the money, it goes to charity.'

'Oh, OK, I get it. We have that at school sometimes, to get money for books and stuff.'

'Right. So there I was, and I was sitting at my table with all these very boring, very rich people who had organised the thing, and I noticed that the waitress, who was bringing our food and drinks, was *exceedingly* pretty.'

'Alice!' said Charlotte. Then she frowned, 'But she's not a waitress.'

'She was sometimes. Her sister, who's called Emmy, has a company called Emerald Catering, and they do food for parties. Alice was helping her out.'

'Oh, OK.'

The bus came and they presented their Oyster cards, Charlotte watching Kit to make sure he did it right, and then climbed the stairs to the top deck.

'Go on,' said Charlotte, when they were sitting down.

'Are you sure you're interested?'

Charlotte rolled her eyes and put her fingertips to her forehead in a manner identical to her mother's. 'Pleeease,' she said, 'tell me.'

'OK, OK. After the auction, when someone had paid for me to paint her – and by the way she was a super-ugly woman, and I had to make her look beautiful and it was almost impossible –' (Charlotte giggled again) 'I was in quite a good mood –'

'Drunk,' interrupted Charlotte.

'Maybe a bit. So I waited until this very pretty waitress had gone out of the room, and I jumped up and followed her.'

'She must have thought you were a psycho,' said Charlotte. 'Then what?'

'I caught up with her and I said hello, and I told her to come to the park with me. She said she was working, but she was laughing, and so I took her hand and we ran off into the park.'

'You? Ran?'

'All right, not quite ran. Trotted.'

Charlotte giggled.

'Anyway,' continued Kit, 'when we got to a tree, I took her tray away from her – '

'She still had her tray! That's stealing.'

'And I took all her hairclips out, and then we... chatted.'

'Why did you have to take all her hairclips out?'

'I like her hair better down.'

'I would hate it if someone did that,' said Charlotte, taking hold of her own ponytail. 'Especially someone I didn't even know.'

On the top deck of their bus, pressing its way along Kensington High Street, Kit did not tell Charlotte about the next morning, when he and Alice had woken and looked at each other in fright, thinking, *Who are you? Have I made a mistake?*

It was more alarming going to bed with someone you liked than someone you didn't, Kit had long since learned. He had ways and means of getting rid of girls in the morning but that day he had saved his tricks. With Alice dressed in borrowed shirt, shorts and sunglasses, they had walked Bones across the park to Chinatown and bought *dim sum* to eat on the pavement, and then walked west along the river and parted on Albert Bridge. Alice lived in Clapham with Emmy, and Kit was going home.

'Will I see you again?' Kit had asked.

'I hope so,' said Alice. As they kissed goodbye, a car drove past and someone shouted, 'Get a room!' out of the window.

They both laughed, and broke apart. Alice bent to pat Bones and then walked away, turning once to wave. Kit leaned on the railing until she had walked out of sight.

But it was not that meeting, thought Kit, which had come to define his relationship with Alice. One encounter of that kind was, in his experience, very much like another: it was delightful, it held promise, but it told you nothing – it could predict nothing. It was only from the thick of it that the temperature of a relationship could be taken and a forecast made for its future.

Now their bus was passing Holland Park, where on another quite different day Alice – who always wanted to arrange to meet outdoors – had rung and said, 'I'll be in Holland Park, in that funny little garden.' She had meant the knot garden, where flowers were planted throughout winter.

Bones thought Holland Park was a poor excuse for a park and Kit was inclined to agree. The dog had to be put on a lead, which she hated, and that day she had trailed behind him wearing a martyred expression, her head hanging, her long nose almost touching the ground. In this pose she looked like a grieving anteater. 'Come *on*, Bones,' Kit had said, tugging her away from the smell of rabbits and squirrels she was not allowed to chase.

Kit too found this place unsatisfying, it being neither park nor garden. It was arranged for the most sedate of outdoor activities to be undertaken either by the elderly or the very young. It always seemed gloomy – dark and still – and the dank ground was greasy underfoot. It reminded him of long weekends with no school, and not wanting to be in the house. Of sitting with cold fingers, killing time until he had to go home.

He had found Alice sitting on a wooden bench overlooking neat beds containing flowers in bloom and framed by low box hedges. The garden was bordered with brown benches like Alice's, all of them memorials, and on hers he read, 'For Robert who found peace in this garden'.

She had been wearing that red coat that he loved and it made a splash of colour in the gloom like a berry against a holly tree. Her hair had been piled on her head and her face tanned by the Florida sun – she had come back from visiting her parents.

Kit had put his newspaper down next to her on the wet bench, and sat down. She was startled – 'Oh, Kit – I was miles away.' She had leaned in towards him, smiling, and he had kissed her on the mouth. Then she had said, 'Hello, Bones!' and bent down to talk to the dog. Bones had been delighted to see her and climbed on to the bench and trampled across Alice's lap, wagging her tail, before clambering down again to the ground where she folded herself in two like a pair of compasses and sat down amongst the cigarette butts with her back to them.

Despite the cold there had been children there, brought out to take the air. The smallest of them lay cocooned in their buggies like royalty and stared out with the same impervious gaze. Toddlers stumbled in one direction or another, purposeless, pitched forward on their toes as if about to topple over.

Small children loved it there because the garden was made in their size: the box hedges were the right height to lean across, or to pat on top with a mittened hand. Anyone tall enough to walk could peer into the flower beds and there were no dangers – no cyclists, or unattached dogs – to make their parents alarmed.

Kit had taken Alice's gloved hand in his and kissed her again. *Alice! Here she is!* He was delighted with her. When they were not together he did not think about her; he could not, for the life of him, summon her up. But then when she was there he could not imagine how he might do without her.

'I *could* live without you,' he had said once, holding her tight in his arms, 'but I'd much rather not.' He was fond of a bold, romantic statement.

He had put an arm across her shoulders and she had tucked in underneath, into the folds of his overcoat. It was a familiar embrace. 'How was it?' he had asked.

'Odd,' she had replied. 'I know what Emmy means… they eat maple syrup with their bacon now. It's depressing.'

'I bet they loved having you,' said Kit, who had a limited interest in Alice's family.

'I don't know. They didn't know what to do with me. One day we went to a water park! Can you imagine?'

'Christ,' Kit had said, alarmed. He thought with horror of having to go there one day and meet Alice's parents for himself.

When Rob had got engaged, and Kit had asked him why, Rob had spread his hands and said, 'I'm bored of dating my wife.' It was the perfect answer.

But when Kit got bored of dating it was because the needs, the hopes and the expectations of another tried to make themselves legitimate, or what was worse, established, in his life. The disappointment, the hurt, the reproach – it became repetitive.

So, one day he might be expected to go to Florida. *But please not yet.*

He and Alice had sat in peace for a few minutes, pressed together at one end of the bench, and had drunk the tea which Kit brought for them from the café. Then Alice had said, 'Shall we walk a bit?'

As they walked Kit had contemplated the day ahead with satisfaction. Sometimes he enjoyed having a girlfriend in a pure fashion, the way he imagined most men felt about relationships most of the time: like wearing the right amount of clothes in bad weather.

This was one of those moments: Alice was beautiful; other men looked at her with appreciation as they passed; the pub lay ahead (there was that nice one at the top of the hill, with a garden), or perhaps they would go home and go straight to bed with a bottle of wine –

'Kit,' Alice had said, 'I'm pregnant.'

He remembered how hard he had fought with himself to respond to Alice in an appropriate way. With appalling clarity, he recalled how he had failed.

'You don't want me to keep it,' she had said in a tone-less voice, snapping a twig off a branch as she passed it.

Are you surprised? Kit thought. But he said, 'I don't know.' 'Am I supposed to know what I want? Straight away?' Then he asked, 'How pregnant are you?'

Alice gave a hollow laugh. 'You either are or you aren't,' she had replied. 'There's nothing in between.'

'You know what I mean,' Kit had sulked.

They had stopped walking and stood on a path with bare trees all round them. Both had their hands in their coat pockets. Alice looked down at Bones, who was shivering. 'That poor dog is cold,' she said.

'It doesn't mean she's cold,' frowned Kit. 'It means she's keeping warm.'

It had been the beginning of a strange formality between them, which they had attempted to cure with that fated holiday.

Kit did not want the baby, he wanted Alice, but he knew he could not ask for that. He could acknowledge that thought now without the creeping shame that had used to accompany it.

All the truth in their relationship had bled away when he started to pretend he wanted to be a father, and she had pretended to believe him. Deceit; the erosion of respect. His was a dreadful cowardice, he knew, and he was ashamed of himself for it. But she must have known how he felt! And yet, with mute defiance, she had ignored it. She had refused to acknowledge him.

That day had not been an event in itself, one with its own momentum, but a turning point. He saw it now as a suspended moment after which life had begun again but been quite different. On that day a resentment, like a dirty fungus, had begun to bloom. It had forced them apart. Bones began to walk between them, on the pavement, instead of at their heels.

And yet all the time they had talked, in fevered voices, about their future together.

8

On the train Alice dozed, woke, stared out of the window, and dozed again. Sometimes she saw herself reflected in the glass, too faint an image to read the expression. Sometimes she saw the passing landscape. Occasionally the two would be combined, as if captured in a double exposure, and she would see trees or buildings flash across her face.

Here on the train in the hanging space between waking and sleeping, between leaving and arriving, she felt content. Neither here nor there, but content. She could gaze at the landscape rushing past the train window, and let her thoughts balloon and subside like sails on a boat.

The train was passing between great green hills, and Alice caught sight of herself in the glass and then looked through the window to the wide landscape beyond.

On the brow of a hill a single figure was outlined against the sky, someone standing still to watch the train

pass, but as the train drew parallel the figure divided:–
there were two people after all – one had been hidden
by the other. Gradually, as the train left them behind, the
two turned back into one.

Alice turned her head to watch this single numeral
recede out of sight. Then she faced forward again, resting
her elbow on the window and her head on her hand.

A CONVERSATION WITH OLIVIA GLAZEBROOK

1. *Where did the idea for the book come from?*
The starting point for the book was always the crash.

I wanted to picture what effect a devastating incident would have on two people who appeared to be, and believed themselves to be, everything that a happy couple should be.

Our society gives so much credit to people for falling madly in love with one another, but is it really such an achievement? I wanted to take those happy, kissing love-birds from the end of a love story (that couple we see photographed in black and white, advertising perfume or diamonds) and put them through a car crash at the beginning of a story.

I suspected it would turn out that such a relationship, if you hit it with a hammer, might shatter into a million pieces.

2. *What were you trying to communicate?*
What Kit and Alice feel at the end of the novel is infinitely more valuable than the glossy feelings they have before the crash.

Before the accident – before they leave home – they seem to inhabit a lovely cocoon. Lying in bed with the weekend papers and choosing a holiday destination is the sort of tempting image that actually appears in the weekend papers – in the style section, or the home section. It is an image that we aspire to – rightly or wrongly – and Kit and Alice appear to have achieved something very desirable. They are gratified by their effect on each other and by the image they project; they are full of confidence; their unity gives them a feeling of power.

But the security of their relationship is an illusion. Even before the crash – just by going away from home – they begin to feel the strain, to realise how unfamiliar they are to one another. When something goes badly wrong – the car falls off the mountain – they are completely unprepared for what happens, both right at that moment, and afterwards. It turns out they are strangers to each other and themselves. Everything that appeared to be so successful about them, everything that, as it were, looked so good in the advertisement – is of no use at all.

3. *Who are we supposed to sympathise with?*
I wanted it to be impossible for the reader to blame either Kit or Alice – neither is responsible for what happens to the other and both are enduring private, incommunicable trauma. Both feel isolated. Both feel guilty and, simultaneously, resentful. Both are struggling to produce 'appropriate' feelings.

Alice is the more obvious victim, because all the bad things seems to happen to her, but poor Kit has just as terrible a time. Alice is so devastated by her miscarriage that she cannot even see Kit, let alone sympathise with him. So both of them feel abandoned and increasingly isolated from the other's experience. They are like two marbles dropped on to a wooden floor, rolling off into opposite corners.

At first the book was written much more as Alice's story but I quickly felt that Kit's feelings and his situation deserved equal space and depth. I wanted the book to be about both of them and their relationship, not just the experience of one. To me he was never simply the 'bloke who can't empathise' but nor was he ever the rugged, rescuing type who would drag Alice out of the car wreck and carry her to safety. I wanted it to be impossible to read him as straightforwardly as that. As with Alice, the more context Kit gained the more I liked him and felt sympathetic towards him. He is just as significant to me as Alice is, and his struggles are just as poignant. They are both, I hope, likeable but defective people with realistically complicated responses to events, both big and small.

Of all the characters, Tod appears to be the most 'blameable'. And yet, because he completely lacks self-awareness, he is, in a way, unblameable. I always thought of him as going along in his own private thundercloud rather like a lorry on the motorway in a rainstorm: oblivious to the trauma travelling alongside.

4. *How did the parents' stories emerge?*
Kit's parents (Tod and Iona) and Alice's (Robert and Carol) always existed in my mind – I knew everything about them, what kind of people they were, how they had brought their children up. But initially I thought that, though their histories were helpful to me, they would be a distraction from Kit and Alice in the novel itself. And then Tod started to bully his way on to the page and I realised that knowing about him was helpful rather than distracting. After that it was obvious that we needed the others too.

In the end Tod became so vivid, and so demanding, that he almost managed to have the whole book rewritten around him. There are pages and pages of Tod, his marriage and his mistress left behind in my computer. I found it quite hard to leave him in the hospital car park and not follow him back to Ibiza.

5. *Why do we learn everything backwards?*
To me *The Trouble with Alice* is a love story, because Kit and Alice learn how to love. But it runs in reverse and

upside down: they fall apart, rather than together.

At the beginning of the novel they think they are happy – they *want* to be happy, they are doing their best to believe they are happy, and the image they project is a happy one. By the end they are both content. I wanted contentment and compassion to be their achievement – a greater achievement than simply falling in love. What they have separately at the end is more meaningful than what they have together at the beginning.

They are most lonely when they are supposed to be intimate. They are most distant when they share the same bed, and closest (most in sympathy) when they talk on the telephone after Bones goes missing. It is not 'falling in love' that bonds them, but falling out of it.

5. *What is the crucial point for both of them in this process?*
It looks as if the crash is the cause of everything that happens to them, but their relationship is not broken by the event itself. It's like dropping a plate that has already been cracked – it breaks along pre-existing fault lines. The way they react to the crash, and why they react in the way that they do, causes more damage to the relationship than the incident itself. So the crash is not the crucial point.

The pregnancy – Alice's announcement of it – might seem like the turning point in their relationship but again, it is their reaction to it that has the impact. Their responses also pre-exist, because of their separate histories. For Alice being pregnant is rescue; for Kit it is the cliff-edge.

The turning point for Alice is when she goes swimming with Emmy and Jory. Her recovery up until that point has been a kind of overture, preparing her for this moment. When she uncurls and floats on the water she surrenders (and when she gets home, Bones is gone). It is the moment at which she accepts everything that has happened, and everything she feels. All notions of blame and responsibility finally vanish.

Alice has three experiences with the sea: the first is floating on the Dead Sea, where nothing is quite real and the water is lifeless. The second is when she sits far above the water on the cliff edge in Cornwall, wishing she could disappear altogether. And the third is this swim, when she is taking part in the scene just like the children on the beach, or Jory or Emmy, or the seagulls: she is back in the world.

Kit has a similar moment of surrender that connects him properly with the real world: when he goes along to orchestra practice with Charlotte. Up until that point he has been trying to keep himself tidy and separate, but here he is, unavoidably, taking part.

Kit also has a false dawn. He thinks that he is freeing himself – seeing off his baggage – when he locks everything away in self-storage and throws a party. But he has faked it – this isn't surrender, or freedom, but another kind of control. (And the industrial 'park' is not a park at all; the ocean of concrete is another desert; the stream he sits beside has been channelled into a ditch.) His fantasy about taking the train to Italy is just as unrealistic as Alice's about living in her caravan – and, in any case, his passport is still locked in the baggage he brought back from Jordan. He hasn't quite understood, yet, that he is not in charge.

Olivia Glazebrook was born in 1976 and brought
up in Dorset. She studied English Literature at
University College London and has written as a journalist,
screenwriter, film critic and book critic for fifteen years.
The Trouble With Alice is her first
novel. She lives in West London.

In case of difficulty in purchasing any Short Books
title through normal channels, please contact
BOOKPOST Tel: 01624 836000
Fax: 01624 837033
email: bookshop@enterprise.net
www.bookpost.co.uk
Please quote ref. 'Short Books'